NJ

The Riddle of the Poisoned Monk

Sarah Matthias

Catnip

CATNIP BOOKS

Published by Catnip Publishing Ltd

Islington Business Centre

3-5 Islington High Street

London N1 9LQ

First published 2006

1 3 5 7 9 10 8 6 4 2

A CIP catalogue record for this book is available from the British Library

ISBN 10: 1 84647 009 9

ISBN 13: 978 1 84647 009 7

Printed in Poland

www.catnippublishing.co.uk

For my children Mary, James, Charlie and Tom

Contents

Characters

Charlie Ferret	an Elizabethan boy
Balthazar	Charlie's cat
Agnes Ferret	Charlie's mother and the village wise woman
Father Hubert	the parish priest
Lord Goslar	lord of Goslar Castle
Lady Goslar	wife of Lord Goslar
Lady Marian Goslar	their daughter
Theophilus Sturgeon	the master chef
Weazel	Sturgeon's minion and assistant
Eadgyth	a cook in the castle kitchens
Erik	a scullion
Barnacle	general handyman
Abbot Gregory	head of the monastery at Goslar Castle

Father Bernard	the monastery librarian and collector of ancient manuscripts
Father Simeon	the infirmarian (a physician and herbalist)
Brother Dominic	Father Simeon's assistant
Father Patrick	the music master and Lady Marian's lute teacher
Brother Gilbert	the keeper of the chalices

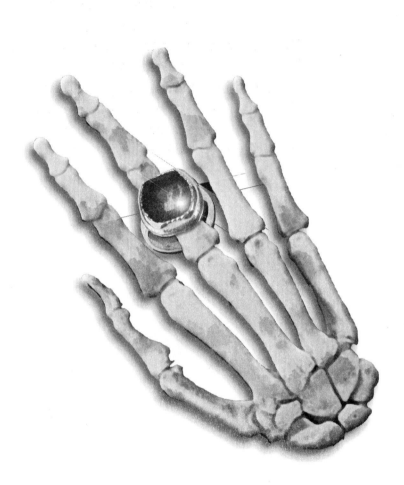

Essex Marshes

31 October 1589

1
The Shape Shifter

It began with a cow. Agnes Ferret, the village wise woman, had been called to a difficult birth – nothing out of the ordinary in that. Sick cows, ailing sheep, childbirth and deathbeds were all in a day's work. But this time she'd made a mistake. The burning feather she'd placed under the animal's nose to encourage an easy birth had produced quite the opposite effect, and a dead calf lay in the bloody straw next to its dying mother. Far from calming the terrified creature, the smell of the feather had sent it into a fearful frenzy, bucking and thrashing against the walls of the small thatched barn. At last, bruised and exhausted, it had collapsed in a heap on the straw. A few minutes later the calf struggled into the world, took one first shuddering breath, closely followed by its last.

Agnes wiped her hands on her apron and rolled down her sleeves. What had gone wrong? It was a tried and tested remedy. Perhaps they were right; perhaps she *was* losing her touch. The villagers gathered at the byre door. She could feel their hostile eyes boring into her back, hear the spiteful whispers of the mischief-makers mingling with the sigh of wind in the autumn hedgerows. Agnes knew them all – the gloaters, the eavesdroppers, the taletellers. She shivered as an icy finger of fear traced a line from the nape of her neck to the base of her spine. It was not the first death this week.

Straightening her back, she pushed a damp strand of hair from her brow with the back of her hand and turned to face them. The cold harvest moonlight flooded the barn, gilding her pale auburn hair. As she pushed her way through the grim crowd, some shrank back for fear of touching her, but others jostled her on purpose – she was sure of it.

The air was thick with suspicion and blame. She was trying to be brave, quiet, matter of fact, but her feet crunched too loudly on the dry beech leaves that lay in drifts about the farmyard like piles of copper coins. It was getting late. Charlie would be waiting for his supper, but first she needed to wash her hands at the pump.

She was just about to grasp the handle when a muscular fist gripped her arm, wrenching it back. It was Farmer Prentice, thickset, red-eyed and smelling of ale.

'Best not touch that, shape-shifter. We don't want our water poisoned!'

Agnes flushed angrily, twisting out of his iron grip. 'Let go of me, William Prentice! Who are you calling a shape-shifter?'

'Be off with you!' he spat. 'My Robbie saw you turn into a hare the other night up on Devil's Barrow. His dog caught it by the back legs as it scampered off, and you turn up here today with a limp!'

'You watch your wicked tongue! I'm no more of a shape-shifter than you are, as well you know. It's evil talk,' she snapped, 'and dangerous! I'm sorry about the cow,' she added more humbly, turning away from the pump towards the farm gate and the rutted track beyond. 'There was nothing more I could do.'

He grunted out of the way, avoiding her eyes. 'Wash your hands in your own stream, Widow Ferret!'

The malicious whispers gathered about her like evil bats, thronging the bare branches of the late October trees, crowding in the shadows under the thatches. She passed silently through the farm gate, past the stagnant pool and out into the lonely lane, the velvet silence surging in behind her, shutting out their spite.

2
All Hallows' Eve

Charlie Ferret crouched in the old church porch and tried to hold back the tears that were spilling down his face and splashing on to his filthy knees. He fumbled in his pocket for a piece of rag and gave his runny nose a hearty blow.

'What a honking, Charlie!' came a kindly voice from behind. 'I thought we had a goose in the porch! What's happened to your nose? Not fighting again, I hope.'

The plump young priest filled the doorway, mopping the sweat from his freckly brow. His long grey robes were stretched tight across his belly and his bright ginger hair stood straight up on his head, as coarse as pigs' bristles.

'Oh, it's you, Father Hubert,' mumbled the boy, twisting the rag between his grubby hands. His knuckles were bleeding.

'Have you been brawling again?' Father Hubert looked stern.

'I won't have them spreading rumours about Mother.

They're calling her a witch again. She's a herbalist, that's all! She cured Eliza Burton's sister and Ellen Wilmot's old cow.'

'Come inside and tell me all about it,' he said, putting a friendly arm around Charlie. 'No point snivelling in the porch. I might even be able to find you a bite to eat.'

Charlie followed Father Hubert into the cool dark church. Rainbow patterns dappled the stone floor as the evening sun slanted through the stained glass. He felt suddenly calmer. His vicious anger of the afternoon drained away as he breathed in the heady smell of the creamy beeswax candles standing on the altar.

'It used to be a lot jollier than this in here you know, Charlie,' said Father Hubert over his shoulder as he led the way down the aisle. 'I mean before King Henry broke with the Pope and all the lovely pictures were painted out.'

It had been one of those golden October days when the world seems to be clinging on to summer, and there had been some hot tempers to match; but the wind was changing. A stiff easterly breeze had sprung up and there was tension in the air, that strange uneasy calm before a storm. As Charlie followed the young priest into the chilly vestry at the side of the church, he shivered with apprehension. Things were turning ugly, and he felt fear in the pit of his stomach.

'Some ale, my child?' said the priest, as he handed Charlie a wooden trencher of coarse rye bread and creamy fenland cheese. He frowned. The boy had definitely lost weight.

'Yes, please, Father,' said Charlie, grabbing it hungrily.

'Come on, lad. Where's that cheeky grin of yours? Race

you with the ale? First to finish gets the last slice,' he urged, nodding towards the remains of the loaf.

The boy smiled sadly. Father Hubert had been a good friend since his father died, taking him under his wing and teaching him Latin and Greek when the money ran out for the grammar school. But Charlie was in no mood for their usual games.

'It's the same old problem!' blurted Charlie, passing a grubby hand through his untidy mop of blond hair. 'They're still saying Mother's a witch and that she'll hang for it. Robbie Prentice says his mother saw her flying through the air and dancing with the Devil; then the Devil suddenly turned into a toad and sat in her lap! He calls her a shape-shifter – says she turns into a hare at sunset! They say she makes wax dolls and sticks needles in their livers and that's why old Alice Hexham died. She knows about herbs and flowers and how to cure the sweating sickness, but she can't cast spells and she wouldn't if she could,' he finished indignantly, glaring at Father Hubert.

The priest cleared his throat, nervously picking some wayward crumbs from his grey robe. He shot Charlie an anxious glance. He didn't want to worry the boy needlessly, but then again it was his duty to warn him. Father Hubert felt responsible for this fatherless boy. There was something about him – a curious sensitivity beyond his years. Father Hubert felt drawn to him, but the village ragamuffins were less sure. He wasn't exactly unpopular, but children could be unkind – quick to pick on differences, and there was certainly something unusual about Charlie that filled Father Hubert with foreboding.

'Aye, Charlie, she knows how to cure a rumbly stomach all right,' the priest replied airily, trying to lighten the atmosphere. 'It was getting very embarrassing for me in church! Those dill seeds she gave me certainly did the trick!'

'It's all right for you to joke, Father. You don't believe in witchcraft in the way they do. Most people see the Devil all around us, inside frogs, cats, toads and – and even flies! People spread wicked stories, and they'll get her in the end, I'm sure they will.'

'I know, Charlie,' admitted Father Hubert with a sigh. 'I'm not making light of it. You're right to be afraid of gossip. The witch-finders have dreamed up some fearful punishments …'

Charlie gave a strangled groan. Father Hubert reddened and wriggled uncomfortably. Perhaps Charlie hadn't yet heard of the witch trials in the nearby villages.

'It … it was bad luck about Farmer Prentice's cow,' stammered Father Hubert. 'Especially as it happened the day after old Alice Hexham died. But the two deaths are quite unconnected. Look, Charlie, people are always restless at this time of year. There's nothing folk like better than to sit around their firesides and frighten themselves. It is All Hallows' Eve after all. Everyone's on the lookout for evil spirits tonight.'

'But why do they call her a witch? They'd never have dared to when Father was alive and we lived in a grand farmhouse. In those days people used to come for miles for her cures for boils and bunions.'

Father Hubert nodded sadly. 'I know what'll cheer you

up, Charlie,' he said with a guilty grin. 'What about a glimpse of the relic? I know you always love to see it!'

'Can I really, Father?' said Charlie, suddenly eager. His stomach flipped over.

'Not a word to anyone, mind,' said Father Hubert, looking furtive. 'You know I only show it to you because ...' He paused, frowning.

'What, Father?' said Charlie.

'Oh, I don't know,' said Father Hubert, feeling along the vestry wall. 'Because you're not like the others I suppose,' he winked, as his plump fingers found the loose stone. He slid a long golden casket from its hiding place. 'The bishop would have my liver and lungs for breakfast if he found me keeping this.'

Charlie watched breathlessly as Father Hubert took a small key from the bunch in the folds of his belly and opened the lid. The boy peered in as the priest lifted the crimson fabric from around a lumpy object in the bottom. Charlie's flesh prickled. It was a hand – the bones yellow with age. On the middle finger sat a huge gold ring set with a blood-red stone.

'Saint Oswald's hand!' breathed Charlie.

'It's been here for over fifty years,' said Father Hubert, 'ever since those wandering monks begged our village priest to hide it for them. It's the hand of a Saxon saint, martyred by the Vikings! The monks fled south to escape King Henry's men when their monastery was destroyed.'

'I don't know why it always makes me shiver,' said Charlie, his eyes shining. 'I know we're not supposed to worship relics these days but there's something –'

'I know, Charlie. I feel just the same as you. That's why I showed it to you in the first place – I knew you'd understand. But the bishop says that relics encourage superstition, so don't forget ...' he smiled nervously. 'Our little secret!'

The light was fading. Through the tiny vestry window, Charlie noticed with surprise that the wind had risen and the trees were swaying strongly against a leaden sky. The great church bell boomed directly above them, shaking the vestry walls.

'Oh, Lord!' gasped Father Hubert. 'I hadn't realized the hour. You'd better be running along now, Charlie. It looks like a storm's brewing and your mother will be worried.'

Charlie's fears crowded in on him again as he sped through the windy churchyard towards the open countryside beyond, dodging the gravestones that lay scattered across the scrubby grass. The taunts of the village children from earlier in the day still rang in his ears. 'Child of the Devil, witch's brat! Your mother's a witch. She'll hang for it!'

He peered through the driving rain as he ran, eyes searching for his own little home in the distance. There it was, candlelight glowing dimly through the rags at the windows. He could just make out the figure of his mother fighting with the cottage door, trying to keep it open and stop it blowing off its hinges at the same time.

'Mother! Mother! You're safe, you're all right!' he cried, sprinting across the clearing.

'Of course I'm all right! Whatever's the matter? I've been out of my mind with worry about you!' She pulled him inside the cottage and slammed the door on the wind. 'Just look at you! You're soaked to the skin!'

Water was streaming down his body and forming puddles around his feet. He stood in front of the fire, sodden clothes steaming. Balthazar the cat was stretched out in front of the glow, but Agnes pushed him firmly aside.

'Get those wet things off at once or you'll catch a chill. Don't forget you have to take our honey to market in the morning. I've promised to take some juniper linctus to old Lily Burdock tomorrow. She won't last beyond the end of the week, poor soul, and you need to get some sleep or you'll never be up in the morning. Besides, we're down to our last candle.'

'Oh, Mother, I'm so glad you're safe!'

'Of course I'm safe! Anyway, I've got Balthazar to look after me,' she smiled, glancing towards the cat, who was busily reclaiming his position in front of the fire.

Charlie lay down on his rough straw pallet. He pulled a woollen blanket up to his chin, but sleep wouldn't come. His body was exhausted but his mind was in turmoil. He felt itchy and uncomfortable. At last his eyelids began to droop as he listened drowsily to his mother's voice. Her sleeping potion was beginning to work.

'Rest now, Charlie. You've a busy day tomorrow, but you'll enjoy the juggling and the dragon parade once you've sold our wares. I've tried to smarten up your doublet and hose a bit,' she added sadly, smoothing the fabric of Charlie's best suit of clothes, 'but they're still looking very shabby, I'm afraid.'

'Oh, don't worry, Mother,' mumbled Charlie sleepily. 'I'm happy to wear my old breeches.'

'You most certainly will not, Charlie Ferret! I'm not having any of those fair-weather friends of ours looking down their noses at you!'

Charlie slept, but only fitfully, dozing and waking, his mind alert and watchful. At first he thought he was dreaming. There were voices in the room. He raised himself up cautiously on one elbow and squinted into the darkness.

'If the worst happens … look after Charlie,' whispered Agnes. 'I'm entrusting him to you. And take my book of herbal remedies. My time's running out.'

Her tones were soft and urgent, but the voice of her companion was like nothing Charlie had ever heard before – a low rumble, a sort of hum, deep and rasping.

'But what about you?' thrummed the voice.

'I can look after myself,' said Agnes briskly. 'You know you can only work for one person at a time. You're Charlie's familiar now.'

Alarmed, Charlie wriggled to the end of his straw pallet to eavesdrop. As his eyes adjusted to the gloom, he could see his mother kneeling by the dying embers of the fire – alone, except for Balthazar! The cat's green eyes glowed in the darkness, as if with an inner fire. Sensing Charlie watching, Agnes twisted round suddenly.

'What are you doing, Charlie?' she snapped testily.

'Who are you speaking to, Mother?'

'Why … er … nobody,' she retorted, casting a furtive glance towards the hearth. 'It's the middle of the night!

What strange fancies you have, child.'

'But I heard –'

'Sleep now,' she said more gently. 'I'll sit with you until you doze off.'

Puzzled, Charlie glanced over to the fire – but the cat had gone.

3
Dragon Dance

The market hall was already crowded with traders and farmers' wives. Charlie pushed through the jostling throng, tripping over pigs and chickens, slipping on patches of goose droppings, trying to find a place to squeeze in and sell his honey. He quickly sold what little he had and began to wander along the main thoroughfare, enjoying the jugglers and fire-eaters. A sudden blast on a cow's horn and a jingling of bells announced the arrival of the Snap Dragon, its huge wooden head painted in vibrant reds, greens and gold. Behind the dragon came dancers wearing devil's masks, banging drums and rattling pigs' bladders filled with dried peas.

Charlie smiled with pleasure and started to jig. The dancers whirled wildly around each other. For a blissful moment, he almost forgot his troubles, when all at once the front of the dragon juddered to an abrupt halt, the dancers behind piling into the ones in front. The drums fell raggedly silent as everyone strained to hear the town crier, who had mounted the steps of the market hall and was ringing his bell.

'Oyez! Oyez! Let everyone hear! Witch taken down by the marshes!'

Charlie felt his throat tighten.

'Oyez! Oyez! Witch taken!'

The revellers took up the cry. Already full of ale and excited by the dancing, they surged forward in a body towards the town crier. 'Who is it? Who is it? Name her! Name her!'

But Charlie didn't need a name. Forcing back sudden tears of rage, he elbowed blindly through the baying mob, teeth clenched and fists tight, until finally the bodies thinned out and he was able to run.

'There he goes, the snivelling witch's brat!' came a cry from behind. A hail of stones stung the back of his neck.

Charlie ran so hard he thought his drumming heart would burst. He paused only to catch his breath and then sped on again, scrambling over stiles and leaping ditches, taking the shortest route he knew to his home. Come on, Charlie, keep going, he willed himself as his legs began to buckle. At last he burst in through the cottage door. It banged back in his face – his second bloody nose in as many days.

'Mother! Mother! Where are you?'

The cottage was eerily silent; the hearth white and cold. There were signs of a scuffle in the soft earth floor. An upturned pot of milk had splashed down on to the floor, but the stain was almost dry. One swift glance around the room and he was springing up the narrow ladder to the floor above. The room was quite empty! He sank to his knees, covering his face with his hands.

'I shouldn't have left her alone! I knew something like this would happen!' he sobbed.

It was as if a moth had brushed his face. He raised his hand. It was something warm and soft.

'Balthazar!'

'You couldn't have stopped them, Charlie. They were too many for you. It's not your fault, but you must stop blubbing. Time is short.'

'Balthazar! You can talk!'

'Of course I can talk, you idiot! I said time is short.'

'But I must find Father Hubert … find out where they've taken Mother.'

'What use is that blundering young fool? You can't help your mother now. But you can save yourself!' Balthazar's hackles were up. 'You must do as I say. Your mother knew things were turning nasty. That's why she wanted you to be away today. It's up to me to look after you now.'

Charlie had no time to think, even about a talking cat. Already he could hear shouting and hammering coming from outside.

'Open up! Open up!'

'Drunken fools,' spat Balthazar. 'The door isn't locked.'

'But what do they want?'

'You, I'm afraid!' hissed Balthazar. 'The village has gone crazy. They've taken your mother and now they want you!'

The roaring and banging was becoming frantic.

'Quick, Charlie! We need to disappear. Do as I say if you want to save your skin!'

Balthazar began to scrabble with his paws in the rushes by the window until he found an iron ring. 'Pull, Charlie,' he hissed urgently. 'I can't!'

Agnes's old book of herbal remedies lay inside a little hole under the boards.

'Grab the book, Charlie. Hurry!'

There was a sound of splintering wood, as the unlocked cottage door fell inwards, flattened to the ground by frenzied charging feet.

'Up the ladder, lads! There's somebody up there.'

The ladder began to creak as pairs of heavy boots started to climb. Charlie could already smell their sweat and their stinking beery breath. He raced to the window in panic.

'We're trapped, Balthazar! We'll never squeeze through this tiny space.'

'Oh, how literal you are, Charlie!' hissed the cat. 'It's a matter of attitude, not size! I've got the tingling in my tail! Stuff the book down your breeches.'

'But I don't understand!'

'You'll understand in a minute when those thugs get their hands on you.' Balthazar was at the top of the ladder now, spitting like a wild cat.

'Strangle that brute. I can smell the witch's brat.'

'Drunken thugs,' growled Balthazar as he flew through the air on the end of a boot.

A calloused hand grabbed Charlie by the right arm.

'Now we've got you,' snarled a spiteful voice.

The cat shot out a forepaw. 'Ouch! God's blood! Damned cat.' Balthazar's razor-sharp talons had torn through the drunkard's flesh.

'We have to jump!' urged Balthazar from Charlie's shoulder. 'Go on.'

Charlie glanced desperately through the tiny window. The countryside looked like a painting – the colours brighter, the outlines sharper. An open horse-drawn wagon trundled slowly along a track.

'JUMP, Charlie! It's our only chance!'

'But the window's too small.'

'Jump, I tell you. Have you any idea what they do to witches' cats?'

Charlie could feel Balthazar's claws digging into his shoulder. The cat was breathing rhythmically now, like a pair of bellows – quivering from ears to tail. All of a sudden, Charlie felt a powerful shiver of sparks rippling down his back.

'Come on, Charlie – let yourself go,' urged Balthazar. 'Don't fight it! I can smell the sea!'

Just at that moment Charlie was gripped by the most peculiar sensation, as though some tremendous force was pulling him in opposite directions. As the demented villager dragged him from behind, something else seemed to be sucking him forward. He felt a stretching sensation, as if his body were lengthening, narrowing, squeezing through an impossibly tight space. The clamour in the room behind seemed to rise to a deafening crescendo, when all at once the din was silenced, as if a door had suddenly been closed, locking in the sound. And then he was falling, falling – plummeting down through an endless tunnel of darkness, leaving his stomach far behind. And now the silence was broken by the babble of strange voices, snatches of crazy laughter, echoes of desperate screams as he sped on, rushing in and out of heat and cold, speeding on down through darkness and light.

Just as he could bear it no longer, he began to slow down. He heard a familiar noise. It sounded like squawking chickens. Then a sudden sharp blow to the side of his head knocked him into oblivion.

'Where's the brat? Where's the Ferret boy?'

The bullies stared around in disbelief.

'He's gone! He's disappeared – and that wild cat with him!'

'I … I had him by the arm and then that devil of a cat nearly blinded me!'

'He can't have jumped through this window. It's too small, even for a skinny urchin like him.'

'It's witchcraft! We know he's the Devil's child.'

The bemused villagers surged down the ladder and raced outside. They looked in the water butt, stared into the sky. There was no sign of the boy – just fat Father Hubert lumbering across the winter garden towards them, his cassock held up in both hands, leather sandals full of mud. Sweat and tears dripped down his plump cheeks.

'Leave the boy alone,' he pleaded. 'For God's sake, let him be. He's an innocent child.'

'You're too late, witch lover. He's gone!'

'Gone where?'

They looked around at each other nervously.

'Er … up in the sky … er … he rode through the air on a garden hoe. I saw him with me own eyes.'

'No, he didn't. The Devil himself came for him, and he flew –flew like a bird, like an eagle –'

'Be quiet all of you,' bellowed Father Hubert.

The villagers fell silent. No one had ever heard the mild-mannered priest shout like that before. Father Hubert squinted up into the slate-grey sky, peering into the distance with short-sighted eyes, half bewildered, half afraid. Minutes passed and still no one spoke. At last the young priest found his voice. Raising his right arm, he made the sign of the cross in the sky.

'Godspeed, Charlie. I'll never forget you.' Tears were streaming unchecked down his face. 'Goodbye, Charlie. God be with you, wherever you are,' he shouted at the empty sky.

Northumbria

AD 1100

4
Chicken Dung

'Are you all right, Charlie?' growled Balthazar. 'You had a bumpy landing.'

Balthazar was perched lightly on an upturned bucket, black, sleek and perfectly clean. Charlie struggled up, gently fingering a lump like an overripe damson on his temple. His jerkin was gone and he was covered from head to toe in chicken feathers and broken eggshells.

'Wh ... what happened? Where are we?' he asked, mystified.

'Close your mouth, Charlie,' said Balthazar. 'You look like a fish! Now, there's some bad news, I'm afraid. We've landed in a dung cart! This wagon is full of chicken manure, with the odd live chicken thrown in!' He shot out a paw to balance himself as the cart lurched drunkenly to one side. 'But the good news,' he continued, brushing a stray feather from the tip of his elegant nose, 'is that your faithful new familiar has rescued you from the clutches of that demented mob!'

'My f … familiar?' gulped Charlie.

'Yes, Charlie. I'm yours now. A present from your mother!'

'But –'

'Your mother, Charlie, is a very accomplished you-know-what. One of the best,' said Balthazar importantly. 'All for the good you know, none of this black magic stuff …'

'You mean she is a witch after all?' gasped Charlie, horrified. 'But Balthazar! They'll torture her – drown her! You must know what they do to witches.'

'Shhh!' hissed Balthazar, glancing round nervously. 'Don't say that word.'

'But she isn't a witch!' insisted Charlie, scrambling to his knees. 'She's a healer, a wise woman. She'd never harm anyone … and where are we anyway? One minute I was standing by the window with the villagers baying for my blood, and the next …'

'I can't tell you exactly where we are,' said Balthazar uneasily, 'but I believe we've gone back in time.'

'Back in time?' gulped Charlie.

'Yes,' Balthazar hissed impatiently. 'It's generally back, but I have been forward a couple of times.'

'But Balthazar!' he exclaimed. 'How can you be so calm about it – as if going back in time is the most natural thing in the world?'

'Well it is – to an experienced familiar like me,' said the cat boastfully.

'But … if we have gone back in time, we'd better go forwards again, hadn't we? If Mother is a witch as you say, they'll hang her, burn her! Don't you realize? We have to get back home right away!'

'I'm terribly sorry, Charlie,' sighed Balthazar helplessly, 'but it's just not like that. I only wish it were. It's not something I have any control over – unfortunately! I do have an inkling when it's time for a journey. I feel restless, fidgety, off my food, that sort of thing, but we can't just go where we like whenever we like.' He shifted uncomfortably, avoiding Charlie's horrified gaze. 'Anyway,' he added with forced cheeriness, 'at least you weren't torn to pieces by that drunken mob … and … and I'd have been roasted alive over a slow fire.'

'B … but Mother …' groaned Charlie. 'If that's what they'd have done to us, think what they'll have … I mean,' Charlie shuddered, 'Mother might already be …'

Balthazar looked away. The wheels of the wagon crunched over the stony track.

'Yes, Charlie,' he said softly. 'I've a horrible feeling she might.'

Charlie stared desolately at Balthazar. A freezing mist was all around them now, sneaking into the wagon, creeping into the crevices.

'Just take a look out here,' said Balthazar in a clumsy effort to ease the tension. He peered through a broken plank in the side of the wagon.

'What on earth …!' gasped Charlie, elbowing the cat out of the way.

The cart was trundling slowly up a treacherous rocky path cut into a windswept cliff side. The sinister bulk of a stone castle loomed ahead of them, high on a rocky outcrop over the sea, its turrets and ramparts black against a dismal sky. A sheer rock face fell dramatically away, plunging down into the surging ocean at its base. Nestling in the shadow of the massive stronghold, secure within its fortified walls, stood a monastery built of fine red sandstone, with round-headed arches and a short stocky tower.

'Look Balthazar – travelling players!' whispered Charlie, as they swayed past a group of strange soldiers dressed in metal tunics that covered their bodies as far as their knees. 'That old-fashioned chain mail.'

'No, Charlie. Those are real knights. Armour has changed over the years, that's all.'

'But how do you know all this? You're only a cat!' said Charlie.

'Hardly!' replied Balthazar haughtily. 'Anyway, it's general knowledge. Didn't you learn anything at grammar school?'

Charlie raked his fingers through his hair distractedly. 'So what are we going to do now, Balthazar? You must have a plan … I mean, for when we get wherever we're going. If we can't get away whenever we like, someone's bound to discover us sooner or later.'

Balthazar was back on the upturned bucket, staring at Charlie with his wide emerald eyes.

'Come on, Balthazar!' panicked Charlie. 'We'll be there in a minute. You must have thought of something.'

'W … well actually …' stammered Balthazar, rather less pompously. 'I … I was hoping to leave that side of things to you. After all, you're the one who's been to grammar school.'

5
Sturgeon

Charlie gazed wide-eyed as the cart rattled under the castle portcullis and into the bustling courtyard beyond. An old man was grinding knives and a blacksmith hammered a horseshoe, sparks flying. Kitchen boys were rumbling barrels of wine and ale across the uneven cobbles. A group of musicians sat under a striped awning tuning their instruments as a black-robed monk hurried past carrying a covered basin.

'Balthazar!' whispered Charlie. 'Just look at these clothes! How can that woman walk in those pointed shoes? And look at her sleeves trailing in the dirt!'

'Styles change over time,' replied Balthazar in superior tones. 'I often marvel at how you manage to waddle around in those funny stuffed breeches. Thank heavens cats don't follow fashion!'

The wagon shuddered to a halt in another smaller courtyard behind the castle keep. There was a strong smell of roasting meat and the sound of clattering pots and pans. The wagon driver jumped down from his high seat, a scrawny bandy-legged little creature in red-and-green striped stockings, spattered with mud and grime.

'Open up in there! Look lively. Weazel wants his breakfast,' he bellowed, hammering on the kitchen door with both hairy fists.

'NOT so fast there, you glutton,' came a voice from behind.

An iron hand grabbed Weazel's dirty jacket, lifting him clean off the ground.

'I want this cart emptied now,' ordered the voice, 'before breakfast! Get it round to the kitchen garden, you lazy scum, and rake it out.'

'Oh, heavens, Balthazar. We've had it now!' hissed Charlie. 'They're going to open up the cart.'

'All right, all right, Sturgeon. Put me down!' cried Weazel. 'I'll do it right away. Put me doooown.'

Sturgeon did put him down – bottom first in the horse trough. Weazel scrambled out looking like a drowned monkey.

'Thank you, Sturgeon!' He was wringing the water out of his tunic. 'No trouble at all. I'll shovel it out right away.'

Charlie crouched among the poultry, trying to make himself invisible. Where was Balthazar hiding? He glanced round just in time to see a black tail disappearing over the side of the wagon as the rear gate was lowered to the ground.

'Balthazar! Don't leave!'

Then came the rake. The terrified hens ran wildly around in the tiny space, squawking and clucking, trying to escape the cruel prongs, feathers and dust flying into Charlie's eyes and nose.

'A … a … a … tishoo!'

The rake came to a sudden halt. The air was white with dust and feathers.

'Well, well, well! What have we got here?' came Weazel's surprised voice. 'Sturgeon! Take a look at this. I think we've got some livestock here and it ain't no chicken!'

Charlie scrambled to his feet gasping for air, limped stiffly towards the opening, slipped on some chicken droppings and fell sprawling on the cobbles at Sturgeon's feet. Sturgeon took a step back.

'Who are you?' he snarled angrily. 'Get up, you brat. Don't think I can't guess. You're a spy, that's what you are! Come to spy on old Sturgeon. Come to see what I'm a-cooking have ya? Who d'ya work for? Thought you'd creep into my kitchen and sneak a look at my special dish before the Feast, did ya? Well, Sturgeon's caught you now, you snivelling brat.'

Fingers, thick as sausages, dug into his neck as Charlie was hauled to his feet.

'P … p … please, sir,' he stuttered. 'I'm, I'm just a boy … Charlie Ferret … I'm not a spy, nothing like it.'

'P'r'aps he's one of them mummers, come to do their play for Lady Goslar,' suggested Weazel, giving Charlie a painful prod. 'What's the fancy dress?'

'I … I'm not an actor … I don't know how I came here … I don't even know where I am. I just jumped out of a …'

'What's the wretch saying, Weazel? Can't understand a word of his prattle. You foreign or something?' bellowed Sturgeon in Charlie's face.

Charlie cringed away from the smell of stale sweat and garlic.

'N ... n ... no, sir.'

Sturgeon's face was slack and puffy, covered in tiny purple veins.

'SILENCE!' commanded Weazel. 'Do you know who you're talking to?'

'Tell him, Weazel. Reveal to him who I am,' ordered Sturgeon, puffing out his chest.

'This is Sturgeon, boy, the great Sturgeon,' cringed Weazel. 'Chief cook to His Lordship ... and ...' He paused. 'Maybe the brat doesn't understand English.'

'Ruler of these kitchens,' prompted Sturgeon, ignoring the remark.

'Oh, er, yes, yes, and ruler of these kitchens.'

'Yes, you young ruffian,' interrupted Sturgeon. 'I am Sturgeon the Great, chef par excellence, and master of this domain. Lord Goslar may be lord of this castle, but I'm in charge here. My word is law in these here kitchens and don't you forget it. Weazel! Take him inside. We've got a whole ox to roast and I'm short of a spit turner.'

6
Eadgyth

A table ran the length of the stone-flagged kitchen floor, piled high with baskets of vegetables, meat and fish. A fat goose was balanced precariously on top of a jug of milk. Men and women covered in flour and feathers were kneading dough and plucking ducks and partridges. Fires blazed around the cavernous kitchen, and over each one hung a roasting carcass – a whole sheep on one skewer, and on another at least forty birds: succulent pigeons, great fat capons and a whole flock of little songbirds. Charlie was crouching at the back end of an ox, laboriously turning the spit. He straightened up, rubbing his aching back. He could feel the sweat trickling down his neck and into his ruff.

'You the new scullion?' A gangly youth emerged from the steam, straining under the weight of a brimming cauldron.

'I beg your pardon?' said Charlie, struggling to understand the boy's thick accent.

'I said, are you the new boy? Hey – don't stop turning that spit! Old Sturgeon'll roast you alive! You must be sweltering in them stupid clothes!' sniffed the kitchen boy, wiping his nose with the back of his hand. 'Where d'ya get them from? Did you come with them mummers?'

'No ... well ... I don't know ... er, maybe ...' stammered Charlie, blinking the sweat out of his eyes. 'Look, you haven't seen a black cat, have you? I've got to find it. You see they've taken my mother ... I don't know what's happened to her ... I can't just stay ... I've been plucking chickens for hours,' he wailed desperately, 'and now I'm stuck here!'

Charlie had been struggling to quell his panic all day long, hoping that Balthazar would show up. He'd tried to shut out all the terrible things that could be happening to his mother while he was stuck in another time. They might have shaved her head by now, stripped her naked and pierced her with a witch-pricker, trying to find the Devil's mark. The witch-finders tore out the tongues of women who wouldn't confess. She could be dead already! Charlie felt tears pricking behind his eyes.

'I must find my cat. I've been scrubbing out cauldrons all day.'

'That's what scullions are here for. You'd better get used to it. It ain't no holiday here – not when there's a feast to prepare. Hey, are you crying?'

'N-n-no,' choked Charlie. 'It's just the smoke. It's making my eyes sting.'

'You don't half talk funny. Look, I can't stop. Got to get this seawater boiled down – we're running out of salt – but if you want anyone to show you the ropes later, Erik's the name.'

Charlie felt a sudden gnawing pain in his stomach. His ears began to fizz, the clatter of pans sounding unbearably loud one minute and strangely faint the next.

'You all right?' asked Erik as Charlie began to stagger. 'Hold on a minute. Give us a hand somebody,' he called over his shoulder. 'This one's gonna fall in the fire!'

Charlie hit the floor. He hadn't eaten for hours.

'There now, my pet, have a sip of this.'

Charlie opened his eyes to find himself propped against a sack of flour, a rosy fat-faced cook squatting next to him with a bowl and ladle. Her straw-coloured hair was twisted up into two coils above her ears.

'Have some of Eadgyth's special pottage,' she urged, loosening the ruff around Charlie's neck. 'You look done in.'

Charlie gulped down the savoury broth gratefully.

'Not from these parts?' asked the cook.

'N ... no ... I ... I don't think I am.'

'Mmm, I can see that dear,' smiled Eadgyth, fingering the bone buttons on his shirt. 'What a good idea these are. Look boys, a little round disc pushed through a hole in the fabric. It keeps the edges of the cloth together. I've never seen the like of it before. And what's this ruffle thing around your neck? You look like something what's about to be served up on a platter!' she laughed.

Erik's giggle exploded, carrying the other kitchen boys with it.

'Erik will get you some scullion's clothes, won't you, my dear?' she smiled.

'Of course I will,' winked Erik. 'My pleasure. No wonder you fainted – trussed up like a stuffed woodcock.'

'But I don't want any scullion's clothes. I'm not planning on staying. I must get home. You haven't seen my cat, have you?' he asked Eadgyth anxiously. 'Quite a handsome one – raven black – bright-green eyes …'

'Mmm, can't say as I have – but you can't go. There's more than enough work to do here. He did choose a rum old day to turn up though, didn't he, boys? Most would have waited until after the Feast was over.'

'What feast is this?' asked Charlie, getting up.

'Well, bless my soul,' exclaimed Eadgyth in astonishment. 'The Feast of the Book of course! Every year Lord Goslar holds a contest to find the best recipe in Northumbria, and the winning dish is chosen at the Feast of the Book.'

'Northumbria?' gasped Charlie. 'But that's nowhere near Essex.'

Erik exchanged a puzzled glance with Eadgyth.

'People come from miles around,' explained Erik. 'Barons, nobles, peasants, cooks – even the abbot of our monastery invented a recipe one year! Lord and Lady Goslar sample all the dishes, and Lord Goslar chooses the winner. He's lord of this castle. Lord Guzzlar we call him,' he sniggered. 'Lives for his food he does. Lady Goslar's worse though. You should see her – almost too fat to walk.'

'A competition, did you say?' asked Charlie.

'That's right,' said Eadgyth. 'It's an ancient tradition in the castle, hundreds of years old it is – started long before Sven the Guzzlar pinched the castle from my ancestors!

Guzzlar's their old family name,' she added contemptuously, her face darkening, 'their real name, before they changed it to Goslar after they invaded our lands.'

'Yeah, and you can't forget it, can you Eadgyth?' said a spotty little scullion impertinently, ignoring Eadgyth's glowering looks. 'You think you should be on the top table instead of Lady Goslar, don't you?'

'And why should I forget it?' snapped Eadgyth. 'I get me nose rubbed in it every day, slaving away, serving them Guzzlars, when it should be me giving the orders! My family was lords of all the land around here long before them Goslars came and took what wasn't theirs!'

'But that was generations ago,' said Erik. 'It's all different now. You're the servant, they're the lords – and we'd be out of a job without them, I say!'

'Well, don't expect me to be grateful!' exploded Eadgyth. 'They're usurpers, they are. Always have been an' always will be!'

'But why is it called the Feast of the Book?' asked Charlie, tactfully steering the conversation.

Erik snorted impatiently. 'Because,' he explained, rolling his eyes, 'the winning recipes are written down in one! There's a precious book in the monastery library, all decorated with jewels and beautifully painted by the monks. Every year the winning recipe is copied down in it by the monk what's best at writing. It's kept locked up in the library and guarded day and night by novices in the monastery – like it was holy. It's more venerated than the Bible even!'

'You'll see it at the Feast tonight,' said one of the scullions excitedly. 'Lord and Lady Goslar and all the family will be there, and minstrels and jesters and such dishes as you never saw in your life.'

'But all this food. It's too much surely?' gasped Charlie, surveying the tables.

'Too much – for the Feast of the Book?' scoffed Erik, giving Charlie a shove. 'Won't his eyes pop when he see the platters, Eadgyth? You tell him!'

Eadgyth was still looking black.

'What'll there be, Eadgyth?' asked Charlie. He was still hungry.

'Well, there's roast ox, braised goose, broiled mutton, poached squirrel, stuffed pike, venison in port-wine gravy, jugged hare, lightly stewed carp from the abbey pond ...'

'And the winning recipe?' interrupted Charlie, his mouth watering.

'Oh, the winning recipe,' snapped Eadgyth sarcastically. 'Don't expect that to be fair neither! I don't know why I even bother entering. Last year, my poached cormorant with crab apples came back untouched; they never even tasted it! Lord Goslar pretends to consider every dish, but sure enough he picks Sturgeon's every time. The old devil wins year after year. Ooh, how I'd like to put his fat fingers through the mincer. You ask old Sturgeon what's going to win!'

'Ask old Sturgeon what, you lazy tub of lard?' bellowed the chief cook, bearing down on Eadgyth brandishing an iron ladle. 'It's you what'll be put through the mincer if you don't stop distracting these scullions – and a lot of mince you'd make an' all!'

'Er, Sturgeon,' came a cringing voice. 'Sturgeon, sir.' It was the monkey-faced Weazel. 'Can you come and test the hedgehog, sir? I think it's done.'

'Is it rare, Weazel?' he demanded, striding off after him. 'It's got to be rare. If it's overdone, I'll boil your head!'

'That brute!' moaned Eadgyth, shaking her fist at his back. 'How can a bully like that cook such divine food? It's so unfair! He always wins – every year. Baked stuffed hedgehog in port-wine gravy with buttered vegetables,' she whimpered. 'It's so simple! A child could have thought of it.'

'Is that it then – the dish he's entering for the competition?' said Charlie. 'Baked stuffed hedgehog?'

'I know. Simple isn't it?' she moaned. 'Why didn't I think of it myself?'

7
The Feast of the Book

Charlie watched in wonder as the kitchen table was magically transformed before his eyes. Feathers and peelings were cleared away and replaced by the most fabulous dishes, a vast marzipan gateau, an exact replica of Goslar Castle, and a huge ship made of candied fruits and covered with shavings of real gold.

There was still no sign of Balthazar and little chance of looking for him, not with Sturgeon prowling round the kitchen, a great iron spoon in his hand, tasting, sniffing and shaking pepper on anyone caught slacking.

'Bearers to their posts!' screamed Sturgeon. 'Somebody bring the peacock – mind its tail, you fool. You there – the boar's head. Erik, where's that new boy? You're about the same height. Take the swan between you and mind you don't drop it!'

Charlie gulped. A whole male swan sat on a pie moulded into the shape of a nest. It was still covered in feathers, garlands of crimson flowers draped around its neck and a golden crown on its head.

'What does peacock taste like?' whispered Charlie.

'Ugh! Really foul. It's tough, and gives you the bellyache. It's only for show. Looks fantastic though, don't it?'

The Great Hall was dark and overheated, smelling of sweat and dung. Even by the light of hundreds of flickering candles, Charlie could only dimly make out the scenes of hunting and feasting on the thickly woven tapestries hanging on the walls. Musicians twanged and thrummed on Norman lutes and skin drums as scarlet and green jesters tumbled up and down.

Side by side on the raised platform Lord and Lady Goslar smiled excitedly around at their guests, nodding and waving to friends. Lady Goslar had once been a famous beauty, but the legendary twinkling blue eyes were hardly visible now, sunk down in the soft white flesh of her podgy cheeks. Lord Goslar, red-faced and breathless, had quite exhausted himself with the effort of waddling from his chamber to the banqueting hall. A quantity of his lunch still clung to his curly beard.

'I can't wait! I can't wait!' squeaked Lady Goslar. 'Ooh, Godfrey, let's get on with it. I want to know who the winner will be!'

'Patience, patience, my plum pudding!' He patted his wife's cheek fondly with a fleshy finger. 'We cannot sample the dishes until they have been presented, my marzipan roll, and then we must wait for the Book to arrive.'

'Oh, Godfrey,' pouted Lady Goslar. 'Don't you love your almond puff any more? I'm so hungry. I only had three blackbird pies for lunch, and they scarcely filled the teeniest corner!'

'Be quiet for heavens sake, Mother! I feel sick already.'

A thin sallow-faced girl with lank black hair shot a sulky glance at Lady Goslar.

'The smell of the food … it's nauseating,' she groaned, covering her nose and mouth with inky fingers.

Lady Goslar gasped.

'Marian! How dare you speak like that! Really, Godfrey, can this bag of bones truly be our daughter? She must have been swapped in her cradle.'

'There's nothing the matter with me, Mother! I'm not obsessed with food, that's all,' snapped Marian, biting her nails viciously.

Lady Goslar's angry retort was drowned out by a fanfare of trumpets. The iron-studded doors of the Great Hall were flung open to reveal the bearers with their dishes, the peacock leading the procession, its tail fully fanned, followed by Charlie and Erik, staggering under the weight of the swan on its pastry nest. Lord Goslar sat forward in his chair making grunting sounds of approval.

'Stuffed breast of veal,' announced the chief carver, 'boiled and garnished with flowers. Fricasséed shoulder of goat with fried shallots …'

'What do we do next?' whispered Charlie to Erik as they placed the swan on the top table.

'Just stand in a line with the other scullions,' he hissed excitedly. 'Any minute now the monks will bring in the Book!'

Lord Goslar rose unsteadily to his feet.

'Lady Goslar, and friends!' he cried. 'Another year has

passed and we are gathered here once more to celebrate our ancient family tradition – the Feast of the Book. Ladies and gentlemen – the Book!'

A thunderous roll of drums erupted as suddenly the hall was plunged into darkness, every candle snuffed out at once. The only light came from the flares in the iron wall sconces and the braziers blazing at intervals the length of the room. An icy draft sliced through the smoke, as the great doors swung open once again. A curious sound of faint singing came drifting across the scrubby ground that separated the monastery from the castle. Small bobbing points of light danced in the gloom, growing larger as the singing swelled louder. An expectant silence descended on the hall. Whispers echoed around the trestles.

'The Book! The Book! Here comes the Book.'

The torches on the walls flared eerily, as the monks processed from the monastery bearing the precious volume. Slowly their singing died away, smoky breath hanging in the crisp air outside. Charlie felt a shiver run down his spine.

The monks shuffled on in pairs: six pairs behind the Book, six pairs in front of it, and four monks in the middle. Each held a corner of a vast velvet cushion on which the enormous Book lay open, its illuminated pages glowing with bright colours and gold paint. The bearers came to a solemn halt in front of the raised platform. For a tense moment, Lord Goslar seemed too overcome with emotion to speak. He took a deep, shuddering breath.

'My friends,' he proclaimed at last. 'The sacred volume is once again in our midst. Let the Feast of the Book now begin!'

As the guests grabbed and snatched, eating with their fingers and picking their teeth, Lady Marian Goslar flounced out in disgust. Nobody noticed her leave.

It was time for the results. Lord Goslar had pretended to find it impossible to choose between a stewed porpoise in juniper jelly, and an eel and garlic pudding for second prize. At last he selected the eel pudding, but not before he had consumed the entire thing – just to make sure! Third place went to a local bee-keeper for his fried honey cakes with saffron and ginger.

'And after much deliberation,' cried Lord Goslar, belching with satisfaction, 'and, er, mastication, our first prize this year has been won by our own chief cook, Theophilus Sturgeon, for his baked stuffed hedgehog in port-wine gravy with buttered vegetables!'

There were far more boos than cheers. All eyes were fixed expectantly on the great door.

'I guessed it! I guessed it! I knew it would be the hedgehog,' clapped Lady Goslar in delight. 'He's won again! Allow me to present the prize, Godfrey, do!'

The drums rolled again, but there was no sign of the master chef.

'Ladies and gentlemen!' cried Lord Goslar again. 'It is with the most enormous pleasure that I now present to you, Theophilus Sturgeon …'

There was a sound of pounding feet. Someone was running in the direction of the Great Hall. A scullion skidded to a halt in the doorway, panting for breath.

'M-m-m … murder! Murder!' he yelled.

The dinner guests gasped. Lady Goslar shrieked in terror.

'Lord Goslar!' cried the scullion, passing a frantic hand through his wild hair. 'Fetch the abbot! There's a body in the stew pond!'

8
The Dance of Death

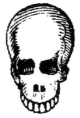

The ravaged body of a novice lay covered in
green slime by the edge of the eel pond, a slick
snake of weed coiled around his neck. The water
glowed blackly in the cold moonlight. Father Simeon,
the monastery infirmarian, fought down the bile that
threatened to choke him. Pity surged in his tender heart
at the sight of the spindly legs, like two waxen candles,
sticking out from under the grey novice's habit. So young
to meet with such a horrible death!

'Ah, Abbot Gregory, you are come at last,' cried Father
Simeon, stumbling up from where he had been crouching
in the sticky mud. 'Thank God you are here, but I warn
you – do not approach too close – it is a grisly sight.'

'Who is it, Simeon? Speak up for heaven's sake.'

'It is the corpse of poor Harry, our youngest novice, my
Lord Abbot! I pulled him from the eel pond as fast as I
could, but alas he expired within moments of me hauling
him from the weed.'

The abbot skidded in his night slippers on the wet grass, ignoring the aged Father's advice to keep his distance. Hastily crossing himself, he stared down in disbelief at the contorted face of the boy, eyes wide open in the vacant stare of death, the tips of his white teeth glistening in the lantern light.

'But novice Harry was supposed to be guarding the Book tonight!' exclaimed the abbot, his eyes searching Father Simeon's face. 'How did he come to be here? Was he not at his post when the brothers came to collect the volume to carry it to the feast? And how did you discover the body, Simeon? What in heaven's name brought you to the eel pond at this ungodly hour?'

'I was strolling by moonlight collecting fresh bark of the slippery elm for my latest cure for the bloody flux, when a strangled groan reached my ears. It seemed to come from the eel pond, so I dropped my basket and made haste in the direction of the fearful sound. There in the light of the moon I saw poor novice Harry, screaming in agony, clutching his stomach and vomiting. He was tearing at his flesh with his bare hands and crying out to God for mercy, leaping like a soul in torment, as if in a dance of death!'

'But Father Simeon, did you not say you pulled the wretched child from the water with your own hands?' asked the abbot. 'How came he to be in the pond?'

'Look to the corpse, Abbot. Clearly the poor child was in the most intense physical torment. Do you not see the ulcerations on his tender flesh, the blood-encrusted rash on his face and hands? And look where his poor legs are exposed,' he said shakily, a sob catching in his voice as he eased down the hem of the rucked-up habit. 'I believe he flung himself into the cold pool in an effort to gain some relief from the unbearable itching of the skin.'

'I see what you mean, Simeon,' said Abbot Gregory, kneeling and holding a flickering lantern above the still body. 'There is caked blood beneath his fingernails where he has ripped at his flesh and drawn blood!'

The infirmarian nodded. 'It is definitely poisoning this time. Of that I have no doubt. It can surely be no coincidence that this poor child met with death on a night when he was supposed to be guarding the Book in the library! Something devilish is afoot, and I believe that this time it is murder most foul.'

'The Book!' exclaimed Abbot Gregory, staggering to his feet, horrified. 'Where is the sacred volume now? I was forgetting it in my anguish over poor Harry. Has it been tampered with? Has anyone had a moment to look?'

'You must attend to it at once, Abbot,' urged Father Simeon, grasping the abbot's outstretched arm and hauling himself up. 'Like you, I had not thought of it in my hurry to reach the eel pond.'

'I will make haste to the library immediately, Simeon, but not before I have sent word to the infirmary for some stretcher-bearers to help you with the corpse. And Father Simeon ...' said the abbot, nervously flicking some mud from his sleeve.

'Yes, Abbot?'

'Someone must break this dreadful news to the novice master and er ... er ... you ...'

'I know, Abbot,' sighed Father Simeon. 'You are going

to say that I am the best person to do it, but I will go to the pharmacy and prepare a calming infusion first. I fear he will take this very hard. He cares for those boys as if they were his children, and poor Harry was our youngest novice after all.'

9
A History Lesson

The forlorn remains of the feast lay strewn about the kitchen; sunken puddings and deflated custards, swiftly gathered up from the Great Hall by ashen-faced scullions. The horrified guests had left quickly, shivering into their cloaks, hastily muttering goodbyes, eager to hurry home and lock their doors. The kitchen was dismal in the dying firelight, the subdued silence broken only by uneasy murmurs and the occasional stifled sob. Gloomy scullions eyed each other suspiciously, exchanging anxious whispers.

'Why are you all looking so sorry for yourselves?' bellowed Sturgeon, striding into the firelight. 'Wait till I get my hands on that measly little scullion what interrupted the feast before I got me prize.'

'Shut up, you selfish ox,' snarled Eadgyth, brandishing a toasting fork at Sturgeon. 'A poor novice has been savagely murdered and all you can think about is yer stupid prize for yer stuffed hedgehog!'

'Poor novice! Who gives a pig's trotter about some snivelling little monk?' snarled Sturgeon, stalking off again.

'It's God's judgment,' intoned a smug nasal voice. Its owner emerged from the shadows where he had been quietly polishing some candlesticks, a skinny hunched little man with a huge warty nose, as red as his claret leggings.

'You what?' snapped Eadgyth, spinning round.

'You mark my words,' pronounced the warty nose ominously, wiping his hands on his apron. 'It's God's judgment. Gluttony's one of the seven deadly sins. This here novice has been murdered guarding that recipe book. It's obvious it's a sign from God Almighty – shows he don't like all this eating and stuff.'

'Er ... sorry to interrupt,' ventured Charlie tentatively, feeling rather out of his depth, 'but why does everybody think the novice has been murdered?'

Everyone turned to look at him, aghast.

'I mean, couldn't it just have been an accident?'

'Of course not!' scoffed Barnacle, 'but then ... you wouldn't know, would you? You've only just arrived!'

'Wouldn't know what?' asked Charlie.

The little man glanced around furtively, as if the murderer might be lurking in the shadows of the kitchen. 'About the poisonings in the monastery library!' he whispered confidentially, as the scullions huddled around him, wide eyed. 'It's happened before, see – but it's worse this time because the poor novice who was guarding the Book is dead!'

'Novices are being poisoned?' gasped Charlie in alarm.

'That's what it looks like,' he nodded. 'Every so often, one of the novices guarding the Book is found in a peculiar state – slumped on the library floor in a sort of trance. There's not a mark on their bodies, but they can't be woken.'

'Are they … you know …?' stammered Charlie.

'What, dead? Nah! Not before tonight that is,' he added with a shudder. 'They're just taken off to the monastery infirmary where they wake up gradually but they don't remember a thing! All they have is a kind of creeping numbness in their limbs. But they get over it soon enough, and back they go to their normal duties, keeping bees an' prayin' an' all that.'

'And what about the Book? Has something happened to it while they're sleeping?' asked Charlie.

'You bet it has! Pages are missing! They've been neatly cut out leaving hardly a mark! It's happened a good few times now and I can tell you, it don't go down too well with Lord Goslar. He's that proud of the Book – treats it like it's the Bible. Shouldn't be allowed, I say. It's blasphemy – and this murder's God's judgment on the lot of 'em!'

'That's enough of that, Barnacle,' barked Eadgyth, who had been listening in grim silence. 'I'll give you God's judgment! Are you trying to frighten these 'ere boys more than they are already? Can't you see everyone's scared out of their wits? Anyway, it'll be Sturgeon's judgment on the lot of us if we don't get this mess cleared up, and it'll be worse than God's – I can tell you that for nothing.'

Everyone jumped to it at once, all except Charlie who

was staring, mesmerized, at Barnacle's nose. Mother could cure those with a dead mouse, thought Charlie with a pang as his own troubles engulfed him again.

'Come on, Charlie, help me wash these 'ere cauldrons,' said Erik mournfully. 'It's the early hours of the morning and we can't get no sleep until it's all tidied up!'

Charlie rubbed his eyes.

'Oh, look at him, the poor lamb,' crooned Eadgyth. 'You'll have to get used to hard work, you know. Come on now, boys,' she yawned. 'Let's hurry up so we can get to bed. We've all had a nasty shock but I expect the Coronation Feast will still go ahead, murder or no murder. That's what it's like here, Charlie. One feast follows another, and old Sturgeon works these boys like animals, he does.'

'Another feast did you say? Coronation? What coronation?'

'The coronation, you bonehead!' said Erik. 'The new king! Don't tell me you don't know the red-headed monster's dead?'

'Who, Queen Elizabeth?'

'Queen Elizabeth? There ain't no Queen Elizabeth, nor never was one.'

'He means King William – Rufus the redhead,' said Eadgyth. 'You can't have heard the news yet. Hit by an arrow in his chest while he was out hunting.'

'William Rufus? But …' Charlie was feverishly racking his brains, trying to drag up his history lessons. He'd always been good at dates. Rufus the redhead! That's what they called William the Second: 1087 – 1100. Eleven hundred! Charlie's stomach turned a somersault. No wonder their table manners were bad! Of course – the chain mail, the long robes, the pointed shoes. It all suddenly fell into place.

'So the new king will be – Henry the First?' he gasped, praying he was going to be wrong.

There was a brief silence. Charlie held his breath.

'He knew all along!' chuckled Erik. There was a ripple of nervous laughter. 'Just making a joke to try and cheer us up, eh, Charlie? But just plain King Henry will do, won't it? What makes you so sure there'll be another King Henry after this one?'

There was a lot of pushing and shoving to bag the warmest sleeping places in nooks and crannies behind the fireplaces. Watchful scullions huddled together for comfort, preferring their backs to the wall. There were bodies everywhere, sprawling in the warm ovens, crouching in half-empty barrels, curled up between sacks of grain. A tense stillness settled on the shadowy kitchen as fearful mumblings died away at last, and a gloomy silence filled the room.

Charlie was too troubled to sleep. The sound of regular snoring in the dimly lit kitchen mingled oddly with the even plainsong of the monks drifting up from the abbey. It was nearly dawn and ice had formed on the water bucket by his side. The kitchen looked eerie in the light of the dwindling fires; huge sides of salted meat hanging from iron hooks cast ghoulish shadows on the uneven walls, like assassins creeping in the shadows, thought Charlie.

Charlie groped under the pile of sacks that he was using for a bed, pulling out his mother's herbal. He could see her in his mind's eye, kneeling in their kitchen garden at home, tending her beloved herbs, auburn hair hanging in soft tendrils around her face. He shivered miserably.

'What's that, then? Can you read or something?'

Charlie jumped. 'Oh, it's you, Erik. You gave me a shock popping up like that.'

'What've you got there?'

Oh, er, nothing much. Just something belonging to my mother.'

'You not an orphan then?'

'Er … no … well … I might be.' He gave Erik a tight smile. 'The truth is I don't really know where my mother is at the moment. I'm worried sick about her.'

'You should be glad you've got a mother to worry about. Not like me,' said Erik wistfully. 'Can you read that?'

'Er … yes …' said Charlie warily.

'You've come to the wrong place here, then! Better go and join them monks. They can read and write and all that stuff,' he said, rolling over on his hay pallet.

'Erik?'

'Hmmm?' replied the boy sleepily.

'You will tell me if you see a black cat around here, won't you?' he muttered despondently, as Erik began to snore.

Charlie felt hot breath on his cheek. 'Balthazar!' Relief flooded over him. He grabbed the cat by the scruff of his neck so that he couldn't escape. 'Where in heaven's name have you been?' He glanced furtively around. 'Thanks for nothing!' he fizzed at the wriggling cat. 'Just disappearing off like that. I've been worried to death.'

'Put me down!' demanded Balthazar savagely. 'I am not a pet cat to be manhandled.'

'If you go off again I'll ... I'll ... go home without you,' threatened Charlie. 'That'll teach you to desert me.'

Balthazar struggled in Charlie's firm grip. 'There's no point threatening me, Charlie. You can't travel anywhere in my absence, which is just as well,' he growled, extending his sharp claws, 'since you seem to have so little regard for me. Now, if you would be so good as to put me down ...'

Reluctantly Charlie released the bristling ball of fur, as if he expected Balthazar to dart away at any moment.

'Most obliged I'm sure!' hissed Balthazar furiously, shaking himself down. 'I think you and I need to get a few things straight. My grandmother is familiar to the great John Dee, Queen Elizabeth's physician and astrologer. I do not expect to be lifted up by the scruff of my neck like a domestic pet!'

'I'm sorry. I just don't want you to run off again. I looked everywhere for you. I've so many questions and ... and ... I'm frightened, Balthazar. There's been a murder!'

'I know, I know. I do keep my whiskers twitching,' he said defensively. 'I've only been away for a few hours. I promised your mother I'd look after you and that's exactly what I intend to do.'

'Then you mustn't go off like that! You're my only link with home. We're in real trouble, Balthazar. We're back in Norman times. William the Second has just died and there's a brutal murderer at large! Oh, I don't expect you to understand, but –'

'Of course I understand, you idiot. We're nowhere near

Essex and we're nearly five hundred years in the past at the scene of a horrible crime!'

'Please let's try to get back home,' pleaded Charlie.

Balthazar growled impatiently. 'I told you when we first arrived here. It's not as simple as that. Your mother and I could never just travel when we liked. We didn't choose the time. The time chose us!'

'So how do we get back? That's what I want to know. Maybe it's not too late to help Mother. And another thing I've been puzzling about – why didn't she keep you for herself?'

'Look, Charlie. Your mother told me to look after you! She didn't want you around – things were getting dangerous.'

'I still can't believe Mother's a witch,' said Charlie in disbelief. 'She didn't cast spells, or use magic.'

'Oh, Charlie, you do have a lot to learn,' said Balthazar disdainfully. 'Those terms are used by ignorant people to describe procedures which cause harm. Your mother's gift is quite different. Her skills with herbs and healing are second to none, aided of course by her splendid familiar, er … that is to say … me! And you, Charlie, will develop the same natural gifts. It's in your blood.'

'But couldn't we get stuck – you know, away from home for ever?' said Charlie in panic.

'Of course we could,' replied Balthazar. 'I'm sure many do.'

'But can't we just try to get home?' said Charlie lamely, the reality of his plight beginning at last to sink in. 'How can you be so unfeeling about Mother?'

'I'm not unfeeling. I just don't believe in worrying about

things we can't change. I'm going to have a good snoop around. See if I can find out what's going on here. And in the meantime, there's certainly a job for a professional mouser like me. Oops ... there goes breakfast! See you later.'

'Balthazar, don't go! Please don't just ... don't you care what they do to witches?' cried Charlie desperately, as Balthazar darted across the kitchen, a black streak after a brown rat, and disappeared behind a pile of logs.

10
Marian

Charlie gazed in dismay at the primitive huts that clustered beneath the castle walls as he tramped on frozen feet towards the monastery herb garden early next morning. Eadgyth wanted some wild thyme to stuff a hare for roasting. All was silent on the cliff side except for the seabirds, wheeling and squabbling over the cloisters, and the cattle lowing gently in the thatched outhouses. The grass was stiff with frost, each blade perfectly outlined with white crystals. The monastery lay close to the fortress across some scrubby ground. As the wind sliced through his thin scullion's tunic, Charlie wondered with a shudder where the eel pond could be.

The monastery garden was surrounded by high stone walls forming a protective barrier between the vegetable patches and the harsh sea breezes. A fire of autumn leaves smouldered by a mossy wall, sending a ragged plume of white smoke up into the slate-grey sky. A stone fountain stood in the centre of the garden in the shape of a leaping fish, its great mouth gaping open. Charlie perched on the edge of the stone basin and cupped his hands together to drink. He spluttered with the icy shock of it.

'But what can you expect if you never practise!' came a cry from a nearby window. 'An instrument can't play itself.'

Charlie glanced up in surprise towards a small bowed window overlooking the orderly garden.

'I detest music! Why do I have to pluck away at this stupid wooden box?'

'But Lady Marian, I am instructed by your father to –' came a querulous little voice.

'Good riddance to my father, and good riddance to you, Father Patrick, and good riddance to this!'

A blow struck Charlie hard on the right side of his face, knocking him off his perch on the side of the fountain. With tears in his eyes, he stared in bewilderment at the broken lute lying twisted at his feet. Its neck was cracked and bent back underneath, and its strings had unravelled from their pegs.

Two minutes later a door underneath the window burst open and a willowy girl stormed out – about Charlie's age, but taller. Her pale oval face might have been pretty without the sullen frown. She wore a gown of soft yellow wool, covered in splodges of ink, with trailing wide sleeves that swept the ground. Her long black hair was scraped back from her face in an untidy knot, but her eyes were startling; a piercing clear blue, like forget-me-nots. Charlie recognized her as the girl he had seen briefly on the top table at the Feast of the Book. She flounced over to the broken instrument, picked it up by its neck and tossed it into the fountain.

'There! He can stuff his lute lessons up his –' She jumped back in surprise. 'Oh! Who are you? What are you staring at? Don't you know it's rude to stare?' she snapped. 'Well don't just stand there gawping like a fish.'

'But your beautiful lute – it's broken.'

'Of course it's broken, you idiot. I've lost count of how many of these things I've smashed!'

'It hit me,' complained Charlie, rubbing his temple.

'How dare you talk to me like that?' she retorted, stamping her foot. 'Surely you know who I am? Besides, you shouldn't have been in my way. It's a dangerous place to be sitting when I'm having a music lesson. I hit the abbot once, but that was on purpose. I didn't actually know you were there. Are you from the kitchens?'

'Well … sort of from the kitchens …' stammered Charlie.

'What do you mean? You either are from the kitchens or you're not. You've got a very funny voice by the way.' She stared at him oddly, as if he were some curious specimen of insect life.

'Where did you get those ugly shoes from?'

Charlie stared down at his thick leather boots, blunt-toed and padded, almost as broad as they were long. He glanced at the girl's feet, elegantly shod in pointed scarlet slippers.

'Cat got your tongue? What are you doing here, anyway?'

'I've come to gather some herbs for one of the cooks.'

'Ugh. Food, food and more food. It's all they ever think

about round here,' she pouted. 'I can help you if you like. Do you want me to?'

Charlie shrugged.

'I'm only offering because I've got nothing else to do, not because I want to.'

'That's all right,' said Charlie.

'I mean, I don't have to.'

'That's fine,' replied Charlie again. He'd met girls like her before.

She knelt down and began to grab clumps of herbs in her fists, wrenching them out of the ground wildly. Their spicy sweetness filled the air.

'Careful there! Herbs are very delicate. You need to treat them with respect.'

She flung them away angrily. 'You should treat *me* with respect. Do it yourself then, if you know so much.'

Marian frowned, wiping her hands on her gown. Her fingers were long and elegant but so inky and grubby, and her nails so badly bitten, that their beauty was completely spoilt.

'Look, don't take offence. It's just that if you handle herbs roughly they can lose their properties, healing powers I mean,' explained Charlie. 'My mother's a herbalist.'

'You'd better get her to make something for that then,' said Marian meanly, stabbing at a great bruise that was already swelling up, livid and red, on Charlie's temple.

'Ouch! Er, yes – I think it could do with a marjoram poultice.'

'Marjoram poultice! Oh, you do think you're smart don't you?' sneered Marian. 'You certainly put on airs and graces for a kitchen boy! Most of them would run a mile before they dared speak to me.'

Charlie felt a compelling urge to explain himself to this wild girl. There was something about her that made him feel sorry for her in spite of her nasty temper.

'I … I learnt all about herbs from my mother,' stammered Charlie. The girl's eyes were most unsettling. 'She's a kind of wise woman. She knows all sorts of cures for fevers and gout and earache. I've just picked up a few things from watching her.'

'Where is she then, this mother?' said Marian disbelievingly. 'You're just making it up to show off, aren't you? Don't you know who I am?'

'Yes, you're Marian, Lord Goslar's daughter. I saw you at the Feast.'

'Oh, the Feast! I didn't stay long there – disgusting spectacle. And it's Lady Marian to you, by the way. Oh, how I loathe this place! I hate all this eating. Talking of mothers – what do you think of mine? What a revolting mountain of flesh.'

'I've only seen her once,' said Charlie. 'I'm new here, you see. I came here in a wagon full of chicken dung. I don't know how I ended up here but I'm …'

Marian began to bite her nails impatiently. 'Oh, go on! Don't tell me you're really a prince disguised as a scullion, and if I give you a kiss your rags will drop off.'

'I'm not lying, honestly. I don't know how I came here. One minute I was at home and then –'

'Oh, I haven't time for this nonsense. I don't know why I'm even bothering to talk to you – only there's no one else.

So what do you think about this murdered novice, then? You must have heard about it.'

'Of course,' said Charlie, frowning. 'It was the talk of the kitchens last night.'

'And now it seems another recipe's been stolen from that stupid book. The Great Recipe Robbery!' she said sarcastically, rolling her eyes. 'Honestly! What does it matter? That Book's like a holy relic, and now it looks like there's a murderer on the loose!'

'But I don't understand. Who could be stealing the recipes, and why would they want to anyway? I've been thinking – maybe it's someone who wants to win the competition, and he's stealing old recipes to give himself some new ideas.'

Marian shook her head. 'I don't think so. They'd know if a recipe had been done before. It's all they ever think about from one year's end to the next and that's the truth!'

'Well, it must be somebody who wants them pretty badly,' said Charlie slowly, picking up his basket. 'I mean, if they're prepared to kill to find what they're looking for!' Charlie turned to leave. 'I'd better be getting back. Eadgyth will want to get started.'

'Oh, by the way, you couldn't make me something that would stop me biting my nails, could you?' she asked, barring his way. 'It's only that Father Patrick likes them short for playing the lute, so I would really like to grow them long, just to annoy him.'

'Well, some rue paste might help. I'll see if I can make some. You spread it on –'

'Lady Marian. Lady Marian! Where are you?' came an anxious voice.

'Oh, no. That's Father Patrick come to make friends. He'd better not catch you talking to me. Silly old fool. He won't understand that he's wasting his time on me.'

A worried little monk in a too-short black habit scurried across the garden towards them, dabbing at his nose with a large linen cloth. He was suffering from a heavy cold and his long red nose preceded him like a fiery poker. His lips were red and puffy.

He needs some poppyhead syrup, thought Charlie.

'Oh, there you are, Lady Marian,' he cried in obvious relief. 'I was beginning to fret. I told you not to wander in the gardens alone after what happened last night! You just come inside now and we'll start that piece again – you'll catch your death of cold. I only meant the sound was a little bit twangy. I didn't mean what I said about a strangled cat! Come along, Marian. Oh! Who's this young friend?' He eyed Charlie suspiciously.

'Oh, nobody, Father Patrick. He's just an upstart little scullion from the kitchen who's been trying to impress me. Says he knows about herbs and how to cure things.' She turned her back on Charlie.

Father Patrick inspected him through watery red eyes.

'Do you, my child?' He dabbed at his nose again. 'It seems unlikely but … you wouldn't know something I could take for this dreadful cold, would you? My nose is dripping like a melting icicle.'

'Oh, come on, Father Patrick,' scowled Marian. 'He's just a scullion. He can't possibly really know anything.'

She stalked on ahead, flinging Charlie a disdainful glance.

Father Patrick stared after her, hovering uncertainly at Charlie's side. 'Follow me, my boy,' he said suddenly, making up his mind. 'I'll take you to the pharmacy. See what you can find for me,' he whispered, as he slipped through the door under the same window from which Marian had flung the unfortunate lute.

11
Ground Mice and Frogs' Legs

'This is the pharmacy, my child. Lady Marian will help you find everything you need,' sniffed Father Patrick. 'We've tortured the lute enough for one morning, I think.'

'But surely I'm not supposed to be in here,' protested Charlie. 'And anyway, I need to be getting back to the kitchens.'

'Oh, don't worry about that,' snuffled Father Patrick, blowing his nose loudly. 'If you can do anything at all for this catarrh, I will be eternally grateful. I don't like to bother Father Simeon right now, you know, not in view of the dreadful … ahem … happenings. He might think me a trifle trivial. And Marian, dear, remember what I told you earlier. Don't go wandering in the castle grounds alone, not until this villain is apprehended.'

He scuttled out, ducking between bunches of herbs that hung drying from the ceiling.

Charlie gazed around at the array of brightly coloured

bottles that stood neatly stacked and labelled on the shelves of the curious room. Dusty books lined shadowy alcoves stretching from floor to ceiling. A row of jars stood on a high shelf, some containing specimens of dead animals floating in an amber fluid. Mother would love this, he thought with a stab of regret.

A rich, spicy odour of stewed herbs rose up from a huge black cauldron that hung in the hearth, its oily green surface bubbling and occasionally erupting, sending globules of the mixture hissing into the flames below. Marian slouched by the bookshelves, sulkily running an inky finger down the spine of a slim volume.

'"The Treatment of the Bloody Flux with Frogs and Toads",' read Charlie, intrigued, squinting at the spidery brown writing. His fingers itched to take down the books. '"Mice and their medicinal properties."'

'I really don't see why I should help you,' said Marian petulantly. 'I have better things to do than waste my time with a kitchen brat, you know.'

Charlie said nothing. The sooner he could get out of here the better. He felt out of place, and in any case, Eadgyth would be waiting. She wasn't the most patient of people. He'd seen her in action last night. He heaved open a heavy oak drawer.

'"Garden spiders' webs",' he murmured, reading the neat labels as he rummaged among the pots. '"Dried cockerels' windpipes."' He unfolded a yellowed piece of parchment. 'Now, this is interesting. A cure for gout – take a live frog, when neither sun nor moon is shining. Chop off its hind legs and wrap them tight in deerskin. Now, that's very old-fashioned! Mother would have used a mouse and some hog's marrow.'

'So you can read Latin then? How can a kitchen scullion read Latin?' asked Marian in a surprised tone.

'Look at these,' breathed Charlie in delight holding up a jar of slimy black leeches in one hand, and one of wriggling hairy spiders in the other. 'Here, hold these a minute!'

'NO!' screamed Marian, jumping back.

The bottle shattered on the stone floor.

'Quick Marian, catch those spiders!'

'I … I can't,' Marian wailed. 'I'm petrified.'

'Oh, for goodness sake! STOP!' Charlie yelled. 'Don't you dare – don't, please don't! It's bad luck. Nooo …' His voice trailed off.

SQUELCH.

Marian's dainty slipper came down hard, crushing the slowest spider. Charlie flopped back on his heels.

'Oh, well done!' he snarled sarcastically. 'I thought you were holding the bottle.'

'I thought *you* were. I couldn't keep hold of it once they started moving. I can't bear them.'

'Oh, it doesn't matter,' snapped Charlie. 'It was a bit of a shock for me actually,' he added more gently. 'I quite like spiders, but I didn't expect jars full of live ones! They're very good for sore throats, actually, dipped in butter and placed on the back of the tongue.'

'You'd better clear up this mess before Father Simeon catches you,' said Marian bossily, but Charlie was already busily examining an empty bottle labelled, 'The Breath of a Braying Donkey', when they heard footsteps in the corridor.

'Ssh!' Charlie grabbed Marian by the arm and pulled her behind a pillar. 'Someone's coming!'

'Why are you hiding?' hissed Marian, shaking him off roughly.

'I don't think I should be here,' he whispered.

'Well, I'm certainly allowed to be here,' protested Marian, who nonetheless remained behind the pillar.

Two young monks with roughly shaven heads entered the room carrying bundles of herbs and a mousetrap. The taller of the two was Brother Dominic, the assistant infirmarian, a sturdy youth with goofy teeth and a ruddy complexion. He hastily threw down his bundle and began vigorously stirring the cauldron.

'What are you making today?' asked Brother Gilbert. He was holding a bloodstained rag to his ear. Sparse ginger hair sprouted from beneath a rather scaly tonsure.

'Oh, just Lady Goslar's heartburn mixture. She drinks flagons of the stuff as you know ... and then I need to grind up some mouse bones. I've that many pills to mould and tinctures to brew this morning. Father Simeon keeps me hard at it. You've got yourself an easy job, I'll say that for you! There's hardly anything to do as keeper of the chalices.'

'I know,' smirked Brother Gilbert. 'It's better than gardening, I can tell you. I wasn't sorry to say goodbye to the turnips.'

'Hmph,' grunted Brother Dominic enviously. 'Gives you plenty of time to snoop around listening at keyholes, I suppose. Hurry up and tell me what you overheard this time, Gilbert.'

The ginger monk leaned towards his companion, lowering his voice. Brother Dominic drew back. Brother Gilbert could do with a remedy for his bad breath!

'Well,' he confided, glancing furtively over his shoulder. 'I heard our librarian, Father Bernard, talking to Abbot Gregory in his room. I, er ... sort of put my ear to the keyhole. The abbot sounded really angry. He said Lord Goslar only seemed to care about the missing recipes – didn't appear bothered about the novices. But now poor Brother Harold's been found in the eel pond it's more than simply a robbery. The abbot's calling it murder!'

Brother Dominic crossed himself hastily and continued stirring the mixture.

'And Father Bernard seemed really upset,' continued Brother Gilbert. 'Apparently he'd lost his temper with Brother Harold in the library yesterday. He'd knocked a jar of crimson paint over a priceless manuscript, just arrived from Rome. You know how clumsy Harold was, God rest his soul! The poor boy spent his last afternoon on this earth scrubbing out the abbot's latrine as a punishment.'

'I wondered what all that shouting was about yesterday. I expect Father Bernard feels bad about it now. I don't expect there'll be novices queuing up to guard the Book tonight, do you?'

'Abbot Gregory's summoning all the brothers to the chapter house. I was hoping to hear more, but all of a sudden the abbot barged out of the door – and that's how I got this.' Brother Gilbert removed the bloody rag from his throbbing ear. 'He knocked me flying and he didn't even apologize. Just poked his finger at me and said, "That's what comes of listening at keyholes!" He looked really rattled.'

'Come with me, Gilbert,' said Brother Dominic. 'This is ready now, I think. He ladled the sticky remedy into an earthenware pot. 'I need to take this over to the castle but I don't fancy going on my own. Honest to God! Poor Brother Harold's cold and dead, there's a homicidal maniac in our midst, but Lady Goslar must have her indigestion mixture!'

'What a ghastly thought!' said Marian with a grimace, as she and Charlie emerged from their hiding place. 'A murderer walking around this castle and we have no idea who it is!'

'I wonder why Brother Harold died when the others were simply drugged,' mused Charlie, relieved that Marian was being friendly again. He was getting used to her sharp swings of mood. 'If we knew a bit more about the novices' symptoms, we might be able to work out who could be at the bottom of it all.'

'Might we?' asked Marian, her face lighting up. 'What fun!'

'Fun?' Charlie looked horrified. 'Somebody has been murdered!'

'Well, not exactly fun then,' said Marian, flushing. 'I didn't mean to sound heartless but ... do you really think you could work it out? We could try to solve the mystery and trap whoever it is that's drugging the novices.'

'Killing them, you mean,' said Charlie with a shudder. 'Who knows? This might be the shape of things to come. I

wouldn't want to be a novice at the moment, I can tell you.'
Charlie looked pensive. 'It's probably a case of poisoning,'
he said uncertainly. 'I'm not an expert, but I did learn quite
a lot from my mother over the years.'

'Poisoning?' gasped Marian.

'I would need to know exactly what the symptoms were,
how long it took the victim to come round and, and ... now
somebody's died ... well ... what happened to him.'

'I'm sure I can find that out. I can ask Father Bernard,
the monastery librarian. He's my tutor. He's in charge of
the main library where the Book is kept. If anyone knows
about it, it will be him ... and I could ask Father Simeon
too,' said Marian with enthusiasm. 'He's the infirmarian.
He's really old and frail, looks like a lizard but –'

'Well, that's an improvement on scraggy-necked old
turtle!' said Father Simeon, scuttling into the pharmacy in
his overlarge black habit.

'Oh, Father Simeon!' stammered Marian, blushing. 'You
made me jump!'

'I think that's what you called me last time I had to paste
your throat with salt and mustard,' he said sarcastically. He
scurried over to the cauldron and heaved it from its iron
hook. It was nearly as big as he was.

'I may be over ninety years old, Lady Marian, but to
be likened to a lizard, really! As the monastery's oldest
inhabitant I should be accorded some modicum of
respect.'

'I ... I was just explaining who you were to this, er, this
boy from the kitchens.'

'Well, I am afraid the boy from the kitchens will have

to go away,' retorted Father Simeon impatiently. 'And I had better escort you back to the castle right now, Lady Marian. Young Harold, our most junior novice is dead, no one can feel safe, and yet here I find you, skipping around the monastery in the company of a kitchen urchin, almost as if nothing dreadful had happened at all!'

12
The Chapter House

There was a subdued silence in the cloisters as the frightened novices were ushered towards the chapter house under the solicitous direction of the master of the novices. He smiled encouragingly at the boys as he fluttered around them, his plump well-meaning face creased with anxiety. His eyes were pink and swollen, as if he'd been crying.

The novices stood respectfully aside, heads bowed, hands tucked within their grey habits as the more senior monks filed through the iron-banded door and into the lamplit gloom of the chapter house: the librarian, the infirmarian, the almoner, the music master, one by one slipping silently into their shadowy places. There was something sinister about the cowled figures in the dark. The atmosphere bristled with tension; whispered snatches of agitated conversation mingling with stifled coughs. For once there was no furtive giggling from the novices.

Abbot Gregory was the last to enter, a powerful man of

remarkable height, built more like a farmer than a monk. Advancing years had added a stiffness to his gait, which he took pains to disguise. Coarse dark hairs bristled from his prominent nose. His lips were full and red and his eyes bright and intelligent beneath their bushy black brows. A murmur of anticipation rumbled around the circular walls of the chapter house as he made his way ponderously to the lectern, his shadow lurching eerily in the light of the oil lamp. He cleared his throat.

'My dear brethren. It is with bewilderment and dismay that I have to break the fearful news that our beloved brother Harold, our youngest and most vulnerable novice, has been murdered most foully and in cold blood. May God Almighty have mercy on his tender soul.'

He inclined his head sympathetically towards the novice master, who stood, head bowed next to the empty place where Brother Harold should have been, dabbing his nose on the sleeve of his habit.

'As leader of this small community is my duty to warn you all. The Devil is abroad! The Evil One is lurking within these castle walls and not one of us can feel safe. He has wormed his wily way into some villainous soul, and the shadow of suspicion falls on the worthy and the unworthy alike.'

His eyes glowed feverishly in the lamplight.

'Every Brother among us knows that this year, drawing fast to its close, has been one of troubles for our community. For many months now our novices have been attacked in the dark watches of the night by an invisible assailant who leaves no trace of his treachery. Our sacred Book has been defiled and our innocent novices struck down. Every night Father Bernard locks the monastery library doors from the inside, ascending by the night stairs to his quarters and yet our novices are still not safe. Locked doors afford us no protection from the invisible enemy.'

As he gazed around at the assembled company of monks, he fixed each in turn with his penetrating stare.

'The friendship that exists among us, brother for brother, is our community's greatest joy and strength. If any of you knows any information that may lead to the exposure of this villain, let him now declare it. Speak up at once, or you will face a sterner judge than I when your time on this earth comes to an end. I charge you all to examine your consciences.'

The monks shuffled uncomfortably, sneaking sidelong glances at their neighbours. A few moments of uneasy silence passed before the abbot spoke again, relief in his stern features.

'Trust no one!' he intoned darkly. 'Let eternal vigilance walk with you both night and day. Keep your eyes and ears open. If any one of you sees or hears anything unusual, it is your duty to inform me without delay. The scoundrel may strike again at any time. Now depart to your cells in peace, my brethren, and may the Lord have mercy upon your souls.'

13
A Cure for Warts

When Charlie returned to his straw pallet later that afternoon, he was pleased to find Balthazar waiting for him with a fresh dead mouse between his paws.

'Balthazar! I do wish you wouldn't keep disappearing.'

'Well, there's gratitude. I've brought you the mouse you asked for.'

'Where've you been?'

'Oh, out and about, keeping my eyes and ears open. I came to warn you!'

'What about?'

'Don't start getting too friendly with that girl.'

'Who? Lady Marian?'

'Yes, her. I know that kind of girl – about as haughty a little madam as I've ever come across. She'll get you into trouble, mark my words. I heard you plotting with her.'

'Oh, don't talk nonsense, Balthazar. Anyway, our paths

are hardly likely to cross. All I want is to get out of here.'

'There's something mighty suspicious going on here you know, Charlie. I'm doing a bit of detective work myself, as it happens.'

'Oh, wonderful! I'm so pleased to hear you're having a good time,' snapped Charlie. 'And meanwhile I have to slave away like a servant.'

'You must learn to take a pride in your work, Charlie, like I do. As a familiar, I'm a kind of servant myself, and yet I still retain my self-respect.'

'Well, my case is a little different. You try scrubbing out cauldrons all day. I'd rather be a familiar than a scullion!' said Charlie sulkily.

'And another piece of advice while I'm here. I'd find a better hiding place for your mother's book if I were you. I found one of the spit boys, Erik I think, snooping around your sleeping area. And how about a thank you for the fresh mouse?' he grumbled, stalking off.

Charlie went in search of Barnacle. He found him polishing serving platters at a small trestle table. 'Look at that,' said Barnacle, holding up a metal platter. 'You can see your face in it.' He grinned at his reflection. 'Ugh! Second thoughts – better not. Just look at me!'

'Er … Barnacle. Now you mention it, I wondered whether – ahem – would you like – ahem – well, you know …'

'Spit it out, boy. Would I like you to have a go at me warts? Yes, I would. How else am I going to get Eadgyth to marry me?'

Charlie brightened.

'Well, I just so happen to have a fresh dead mouse in my

pocket!' he grinned, fishing it out, and swinging it around by its tail.

'Now, hold still … no, I mean really still.'

'But I can't breathe! I'm suffocating. Ugh, the pong!'

The treatment of Barnacle's warts had begun, and a large audience had gathered. Even Weazel had left Sturgeon's side for just a minute and was having a good gawp. Charlie consulted his herbal again. He was keeping it close by his side, away from prying fingers.

'Now, hold still for half an hour.'

'Half an hour!' groaned Barnacle.

'It's not very long – it'll be worth it – now I mean still.'

'But its blood's dripping down me chin!'

'It's all part of the cure. It has to be a fresh mouse. Nothing else will do. Do you want to get rid of the warts or not?'

Barnacle looked pitiful – slumped on a stool, his head twisted to one side and half a dead mouse balanced on the left-hand side of his nose.

'Won't make any difference, Barnacle,' said Erik with a sly smile. 'Eadgyth'll never marry you. Anyway, what's the point of having half a nose without warts? What about the other half?'

'We'll do the other half if this half works,' replied Charlie tartly.

'Take no notice, Charlie,' mumbled Barnacle from under the mouse. 'When this is done I'll be as handsome as a prince! You mark my words. Eadgyth'll be making me honey cakes and saffron whirls and begging me to marry her!'

Barnacle began to chuckle and Charlie had to dive for the mouse which was beginning to slip off.

'You must keep still. We need as much of the mouse in contact with the warts for as long as possible.'

'Then what?' grimaced Barnacle.

'Then I go and bury the mouse in the ground. As the mouse begins to rot, the warts should disappear,' replied Charlie doubtfully.

He was feeling extremely nervous. He'd never tried to cure warts before. Why hadn't he started with something simple, like pimples?

'What's a-goin' on here?' bellowed Sturgeon.

'Er, Sturgeon, sir.' Weazel was scuttling around Sturgeon's legs, tripping over his own feet. 'It's the new scullion, sir, Charlie Ferret. He's causing trouble, distracting everybody. I was just coming to tell you.'

'What's that on your face, Barnacle? Stand up you ugly brute – answer me!'

Barnacle knocked over his stool in his haste to obey, the mouse flying through the air.

'I'd … I'd finished me work, sir, and Charlie, you know, the new scullion, sir, well he was helping me with me problem.'

'Problem?' growled Sturgeon growing purple, the thick veins at the sides of his neck pulsing dangerously.

'Erm, you know, me warts. Charlie says he can get rid of 'em …' he trailed off.

'I'll tell you what I can to get rid of!' he roared, picking Barnacle up in one of his meaty hands, like a rag doll. Barnacle hung in the air, legs wildly pumping.

'Weazel! Take the lid off that there vat of pickled onions – I've got another one to add!'

There was an enormous splash, followed by yells and splutters and the sound of floundering, as Barnacle struggled to get out of the vat with the help of a few kind-hearted scullions.

'Now, I've got a nice little job for a couple of you,' snarled Sturgeon. 'Who's it to be, then?' He glowered round at the boys who were all trying to make themselves invisible. 'Yes,' he drawled, 'you, the new boy, and ... let me see now ... Erik! I need two "volunteers". The cesspits need cleaning out.'

'It's usually worse than this,' said Erik through a greasy bandage that he'd wrapped around his nose and mouth. 'It's so cold, all the dung's gone hard. Now imagine it here on a hot summer's day!'

Charlie and Erik shovelled the evil-smelling mess from the pits into a handcart and trundled it to the cliff top, tipping it over into the foaming sea below. Charlie retched. The stench was overpowering.

'I can't imagine it worse than this,' said Charlie, breathing hard through his mouth. 'Sturgeon's a mean old brute. How would he like to do it?'

'Yeah. Things would be a lot better in the kitchens if Eadgyth was in charge.'

'I think we've finished,' gasped Charlie, still pinching his nose between his thumb and forefinger. 'You wheel the barrow over and I'll put the shovels back.'

Charlie rubbed his aching back.

'Psst, psst. Up here, Charlie!'

Charlie looked up. The cesspit came out immediately at the foot of the castle walls, so Charlie had to step back and squint up to see where the sound was coming from.

'It's me, Marian. Can you come up? There's a spiral staircase over to your left under an arch – seventy-nine steps and you're here.'

'But I –'

'Oh, come on, I've got things to tell you.'

Charlie looked round quickly to check that Erik wasn't watching him.

'I can't – I'm with somebody.'

Charlie turned away, just as Erik came trundling back with the empty handcart.

'Er … Erik … I forgot. I've just got to go to the herb garden to get some rosemary. I promised Eadgyth. You take the handcart back.'

'Righto, Charlie.'

Charlie bent down and pretended to fiddle with his boots until Erik passed out of sight around the edge of the castle wall.

'Marian!' he hissed.

'Yes, I'm still here. Come on up. Hurry! I need to speak to you urgently. I've found something out!'

14
An Itchy Rash

'You're filthy!' Marian clapped an inky hand over her mouth and nose.

'You would be too if you'd been shovelling muck out of a latrine.'

'Ugh, is that what you were doing?' She wrinkled up her nose. 'I suppose you must be used to it.'

'Of course I'm not used to it!' spluttered Charlie in indignation. 'I haven't always been a –'

'Look, I've got to be quick,' said Marian hurriedly. 'I had the most awful lecture from Father Simeon about being seen with a scullion the other day.'

'What have you found out?' asked Charlie. 'I've got to get back too, or Sturgeon'll be on the warpath.'

'Well, the recipes are always stolen on the night after a full moon,' said Marian excitedly. 'At least, it's happened seven times and seven recipes have been cut out of the Book – always from the front of the book where the most ancient recipes are inscribed. Now, on six of those nights there'd been a full moon the night before.'

'Who told you all this?'

'Father Simeon! The infirmarian. You know,' she giggled, 'the old lizard you met the other day in the pharmacy. He's kept a note of all the dates when the monks were found drugged and a recipe taken. It was always just after a full moon, except for this last time – you know, when that novice died.'

'How do you know you can trust Father Simeon?'

'Trust Father Simeon?' Marian looked crestfallen. 'Of course I can trust him! He's the cleverest doctor ever – and the kindest. He's been here all his life. He was left as an orphan on the monastery steps when he was a baby. He lives for the abbey.'

'Yes, and he's the head of the infirmary. Some herbs are very dangerous, Marian. They need to be handled with care. He might be the only person in the monastery who knows which they are and where they're kept.'

'Oh, nonsense,' snorted Marian, frowning. 'Lots of monks help in the infirmary. Brother Dominic's his assistant – it could be him! You'll be suspecting Father Bernard next because he's the librarian and the novices were found drugged in the library! He's been my tutor since I was a little girl. These monks are like my family, Charlie – more than my real mother and father. I spend more time with the monks than I do at the castle.'

'I'm not accusing anybody Marian, but we have to be suspicious of everyone until this villain is found. Have you forgotten what that ginger monk said about Father Bernard – when we were hiding in the pharmacy? He'd had a blazing row with poor Brother Harold the day he died – over a priceless manuscript! Think what a ruined manuscript would mean to a librarian who spends his entire life looking after books!'

Marian looked dejected.

'What's the matter, Marian?'

'It's just that … well, I have lessons in Father Bernard's room above the library. I know it well. There's a staircase leading directly from his room down to the library below!'

'See what I mean?' said Charlie with satisfaction. 'Trust no one. But we mustn't jump to hasty conclusions either.' He shivered. Marian was snuggled in a fur-lined cloak.

'What was wrong with the novices when they were found? What did Father Simeon say?'

'Well, they were all taken to the infirmary. They were very drowsy, almost as if they were drunk. They had a high fever and numbness in their hands and feet. But Brother Harold, the novice who died – he was different. He was in a lot of pain,' said Marian solemnly. 'Dreadful stomach cramps, vomiting – and he was covered in an itchy rash all over his body. He was in such agony, he flung himself into the eel pond.' Marian looked triumphantly at Charlie. 'You must be frozen.'

'Yes, I am a bit cold,' replied Charlie enviously. 'Numbness, did you say?'

'Yes, so what do you think? You said you knew all about herbal medicine.'

'Yes, but not about poisoning. My mother's a wise woman, not a poisoner!'

'Look it up in your book, then.'

'Oh, the herbal's no good. We need a book about poisonous plants, that kind of thing. You'll have to go and look in the monastery library.'

'Me?' exclaimed Marian.

'Well, I can't! How can a scullion get into the library?'

'Charlie! There's a murderer about, and you tell me to go to the very place where he last struck – and alone!' She shuffled uncomfortably. 'I'm not that good at reading anyway.'

'But you're a Lady. You must be able to read.'

Marian shrugged. 'Well, I can a bit, but I've never really bothered with it. I know my letters but …' she broke off and stood chewing her bitten nails. 'So you see it has to be you.'

'Well, that's just great!' replied Charlie impatiently. 'You can hardly read and I can't get into the library, so we're completely stumped. Look, I've got to go back.' He turned to leave.

'No wait … WAIT!' Marian stamped her foot. 'You can't just go like that! I've been trying to see you for ages! Look, there might be a way. You can get into the library through the church. There's a door in the choir stalls that leads to a passage to the library. There are monks in the library all day, so we'd have to go at night and during a service when the church is unlocked – matins or something – that's about two o'clock in the morning.'

'Oh this is stupid!' snapped Charlie. 'We'd be seen, and what if I was found in the library? They'd think I was the murderer! I've got problems of my own, you know!

They're suspicious of me in the kitchens already because I'm different.'

'Look, how else are we going to find out?' wheedled Marian. 'Don't you even want to try? I'll bring you a cloak, a black cloak, so you won't be recognized. We'll sneak in before the monks arrive. We'll need candles and ... and a tinderbox. All the monks will be at matins and we'll have the library to ourselves.'

Oh, great! Just us and the poisoner! thought Charlie – but he was weakening. 'I'll have to think of an excuse to get away.'

'No, you won't – not at night. Just wait until everyone's asleep and sneak out. I'll be waiting in the monastery garden, by the fountain. Say you'll do it, Charlie. Please. I'll bring you a cloak – I promise.'

15
The Secret Door

C harlie winced as the great oak door creaked on its rusty hinges. He paused for a second to cast a wary glance around the slumbering kitchen, before softly pulling it shut behind him. Armed with two mutton-fat candles and a small tinderbox, he began to walk silently towards the monastery garden, away from the brooding bulk of the castle. The moon emerged from behind the scudding clouds, casting a gloomy shadow of battlements across his path.

It was colder than ever. Gazing out to sea, Charlie could see the rain blowing across the horizon in icy grey sheets. He turned in under the sandstone arch in the wall of the herb garden and made straight for the fountain where Marian had suggested they meet. A black hooded figure emerged from the shrubbery, clutching a bundle. Charlie sighed with relief. She'd remembered the cloak as well!

'It belongs to Father. I hope it's all right. He's short but very fat,' giggled Marian.

Charlie snuggled into the delicious warmth of the soft black fur and pulled up the hood. The cloak was much too big for him, but he wasn't complaining.

'I've brought two candles and something to light them with,' he said. 'What are we going to do now?'

'Exactly what we planned. Get into the library through the church and have a look for a book on poisoning. Come on. We've got to be quick. I've found out that they open the church doors a little before matins. After that, we've got about ten minutes to slip into the choir stalls and find the door that leads to the passage. Now, follow me. I'm going to keep off the main paths.'

As Charlie turned back to disentangle his cloak from a holly bush, he saw a thin black shadow dart across behind him. Balthazar! Checking up on me, I expect, thought Charlie.

The church door was open. Slipping inside, they were dazzled by the light and silence. Tall beeswax candles flickered on the altar. Charlie felt a sudden stab of sadness – it reminded him of the old church at home. Slender pillars soared up all around, their supporting arches stretching into the dusky shadows, beyond the radiance of the candlelight. Marian tugged at his cloak.

'Come on! What are you staring at? Let's go.' She scampered up the nave and began to sidle into the choir stalls. 'Hurry up. I can hear footsteps!'

Charlie could hear them too, the soft shuffling of the monks' sleepy feet as, newly roused from their beds, they processed wearily into the nave. Charlie was right behind, squeezing in next to Marian, who was already groping frantically for the secret door. Balthazar crouched in the shadows, silently watching, his emerald eyes glistening in the gloom.

'I can't find the latch! You'll have to light a candle,' whispered Marian.

There wasn't time to light one of his own so, kneeling down to avoid being seen, Charlie reached up above his head and wiggled a lighted candle out of its holder at the end of the choir stalls, bringing down a shower of molten wax on his hands and hair.

'Ouch!'

'Ssh!'

'I've just been scalded with boiling wax, but not to worry!' Charlie hissed back.

'Oh thank goodness, here it is,' muttered Marian in relief.

She lifted the latch, but the door wouldn't budge. She turned in alarm to Charlie.

'It's locked!' she mouthed.

In despair, she crouched down next to him, balancing the candle between them.

'They're bound to find us now,' she panicked. 'What are you doing, Charlie?'

Charlie was squinting at a shadowy carving underneath one of the choristers' seats: a dragon-headed Viking ship, with a row of circular shields arranged down its side. Unseen by Marian, Balthazar darted soundlessly into the folds of his cloak.

'Look, Balthazar!' he whispered, suddenly aware of the cat. 'Do you see that?'

Charlie narrowed his eyes in the gloom. The wooden ship seemed to be moving, lurching on a storm-wracked sea. Was it only his imagination or could he feel a salty wind on his cheeks? As he sank his fingers into Balthazar's soft black fur, a feeling of pins and needles fizzed through his body. The blood began to throb in his ears, gently at first but growing louder – then through the rhythmic thrumming in his head came the chilling noise of battle. 'Don't leave me, Balthazar!' he begged, as an inky blackness washed right over them, shutting out the candlelight.

'Charlie!' breathed Marian. 'What's the matter? Charlie – speak to me!' she pleaded.

Charlie lay slumped on his side in the narrow choir stalls. He'd knocked over the candle. Marian could hardly see. She reached out her hand to touch him in the darkness, relieved to feel the warm fur of his cloak. She edged closer, grasping the fabric, but the fur seemed to melt at her touch, leaving her fingers hot and tingling.

'Oh, heavens, whatever's happened?' she gasped in disbelief.

Charlie had completely disappeared.

Northumbria

AD 790

16
Abbot Oswald

'God's blood! What devilish place this time?' cried Balthazar, quivering with horror. He sprang to his feet, hackles raised. 'It sounds like the gates of hell!'

Charlie scrambled up from the rough floor where he'd landed. He stared wildly around in terror, ears ringing with the blood-curdling screams from outside the walls of a small thatched chapel. They cowered together, listening with rising panic to the relentless clash of sword on sword mingling with the cries of terrified animals and people.

'The Northmen are coming!' came anguished cries. 'The dragon ships are here!'

The door of the Saxon church burst open and two petrified monks charged towards the altar, grabbed the golden cross and chalice and stuffed them into a sack. A third drew a thick wooden bar across the door behind them, making the sign of the cross as he raced to join the others. Almost at once there was a thunderous pounding. A few seconds later and the door fell in with a scream of splintering wood.

'Get down, you fool!' hissed Balthazar, urgently clawing at Charlie's sleeve and dragging him behind a bench.

Two flaxen-bearded warriors leapt roaring in, wild matted hair escaping from beneath their helmets. As they advanced upon the three shaven-headed monks, one of the brothers fell to his knees, his hands clasped above his head as if in prayer, pleading for mercy. The kneeling monk was slaughtered with one swift slash of a double-headed axe. Undaunted, the two remaining brothers lunged towards the warriors, one brandishing a cross, the other a golden goblet. Charlie and Balthazar crouched petrified in their hiding place as the brave monks were hacked limb from limb. Seizing the sacks, the two murderers fled, their war whoops echoing eerily around the desecrated chapel.

Charlie peered cautiously over the back of the bench. His stomach rose to his mouth at the sight of the grisly remains of the three monks lying strewn about the nave. Blood lay in pools, already beginning to congeal.

'What gruesome place is this, Balthazar?' gasped Charlie, covered in gooseflesh. He could smell burning and hear the crackle of flames outside. 'I thought we were going to be caught in the choir stalls.'

'Caught in the choir stalls!' exploded Balthazar. 'Ever heard the saying "Out of the frying pan ..."'

Charlie's eyes were wide with terror. 'I'm scared, Balthazar!'

'Of course you're scared! We're in the middle of a battle,

in case you hadn't noticed, and goodness only knows what time and place this is!'

Charlie had just begun to edge out of his narrow hiding place when a door behind the altar opened, and two figures emerged, deep in earnest conversation. They were talking rapidly in tones of barely suppressed panic. Charlie shrank back, pushing Balthazar down.

One of the pair was strongly built but slender, not young but curly-haired and handsome with the noble bearing of a lord. He wore a knee-length tunic, his cloak caught up at the shoulder with a jewelled brooch. His companion was an elderly abbot, robed in austere black, his only ornament a heavy golden cross, inlaid with a deep amber stone, which hung from his leather belt.

'I can smell burning,' whispered Charlie in a strangled voice. 'We must get out!'

'Stay where you are, Charlie,' warned Balthazar in low tones. 'They look friendly enough but you never know with humans!'

'God's wounds!' cried the abbot, recoiling in revulsion at the sight of the bloody remains of the slaughtered monks. 'May Heaven reward them for their sacrifice,' he murmured, kneeling down beside the bodies on the bloody earth, his voice catching in his throat.

'We shall probably all be slain, Abbot Oswald,' said the handsome lord urgently, pulling at his robe. 'But we must defend ourselves from these pagans as long as we have breath. Get up, my Lord Abbot. Let the dead bury their dead. Our time is running out!'

'You're right about the smell, Charlie,' whispered

Balthazar. 'Those two don't seem to have noticed. I think the thatch is on fire! We'd better run for it, after all.'

Smoke was curling in the rafters, rapidly snaking its way along the rough timbers of the roof.

'Shhh!' hissed Charlie, shaking him off.

'But we'll be burnt alive!'

'Shhh! Listen, I tell you –'

'I will not allow these pagans to seize all our treasures,' continued the noble lord breathlessly. 'I have gathered together altar pieces and all our holy relics and concealed them in a secret place, which I will not tell even you, Abbot Oswald. If you are captured, you can swear you know nothing, and your conscience will be clear. But this I give to you for safe keeping.'

Charlie craned his neck. The nobleman held a large golden ring in his hand, set with a blood-red stone.

'The smoke, Charlie,' wheezed Balthazar. 'It's getting worse. I can hardly breathe! We must get out now!'

'Not yet! I must hear this. I know it's important – don't ask me why.'

'Guard this ring as you would a holy relic,' urged the nobleman, coughing as the smoke descended from the rafters. 'If I am killed, this jewel holds the key to where our sacred treasures can be found.' He slid the nail of his thumb around the heavy gold setting. It sprang up to reveal a cavity beneath. 'The parchment within this ring contains a runic riddle. Solve it and the secret hiding place will be disclosed. Now, take it, my friend.'

The abbot's eyes were bright with tears as he slipped the ring on to his finger.

'And now farewell, Abbot Oswald. I would rather die than be a slave to these heathens!' cried the Saxon lord, striding defiantly down the murky nave of the little church, picking his way between the bloody remains of the slaughtered monks.

Charlie and Balthazar could bear the smoke no longer. Flames were licking their hungry way along the timbers of the roof, black ash falling like filthy rain.

'Fire!' choked Charlie, as he stumbled from his hiding place. 'I can't breathe! Fire! Fire!'

If the abbot felt surprise at seeing the boy and the cat, he showed none.

'Through this door, Charlie,' he coughed urgently. 'This way, my child. You were brave to remain hidden for so long, but now we must fly. I fear the roof is about to fall!'

17
The Amber Cross

'Stay with me, Balthazar!' wheezed Charlie.

As they followed the old abbot through the door behind the altar, they heard the first flaming timbers from the blazing roof crash down behind them. Outside the chapel a great barn blazed to the east, huge flames licking the sky with tongues of scarlet and orange. Fork-bearded warriors were herding unarmed monks like cattle, driving them down towards the seashore where the dragon-prowed ships lay waiting, drawn up on the shelving sandy beach.

At least twenty slender square-sailed ships lay at anchor a little offshore, battle banners furling in the wind. The sea boiled with warriors surging from the ships, wading through the foaming waves towards the shore, helmets glittering with reflected light from the fires that raged through the settlement.

'Quick – this way!' commanded the abbot, scurrying behind a haystack. 'Make for the blacksmith's in the clearing! Look out!'

A ferocious warrior leapt towards Charlie, wielding a fiery brand. Bright blood oozed from beneath his helmet, but his eyes were on a group of monks who crept stealthily towards the trees with some bulky sacks. With a scream of triumph, he gave chase over the sandy tussocks and into the woods after the terrified monks.

The blacksmith's hut was warm and smoky. A brazier smouldered in the gloom, casting an eerie light on the stone water trough and row of iron horseshoes that hung from nails on the wall. Abbot Oswald hastily pulled the wooden door closed behind them.

'Who … who are you?' gasped Charlie. 'Back there in the burning chapel – you called me by name!' he stammered, glancing round for Balthazar who was hiding behind a leather bucket. 'God help me! There's a massacre going on outside!'

'Welcome, my brave child,' said the abbot gravely, grasping Charlie firmly by the shoulders. The firelight sparkled on the blood-red stone on his finger.

'I'm … I'm not brave at all. I'm terrified!' whimpered Charlie desperately, wiping the sweat from his stinging eyes. 'Who are you?'

'I am Oswald, abbot of this monastery … or I was once,' he replied bitterly. 'But it is over now.'

Outside the hut a horse screamed in pain.

'A … abbot Oswald?' stammered Charlie, stabbed by a sudden painful memory of home. 'And … and who are these warriors?'

'They are barbarians from across the sea. Last time

they seized only a few treasures, but even that raid left the church spattered with the blood of our priests. We have lived in constant fear of their return.'

Charlie cried out in panic, clutching the abbot's robe.

'Courage, my child. Listen to me,' he continued urgently. 'You are no ordinary boy! I know you for what you are – a wanderer through time. I sensed you in the burning church. There is much you can do to help us in our darkest hour. You can be our messenger – the one to take the knowledge that this ring contains to safety.'

'But what has this to do with me? I told you, I'm not brave, I'm just a –'

'Bravery is not the absence of fear, my child. A fearless man is not brave, only foolish!'

'I … I don't understand,' stammered Charlie.

'You must trust me,' said the abbot insistently, raising his voice above the whinnying of pain from beyond the walls. 'There is a purpose to everything, and as you grow in wisdom you will understand. You overheard what was said about this ring?'

'I … I … didn't mean to eavesdrop.'

'Listen carefully to what you must do. Take this ring. Use the secret that it contains with wisdom. You will know when the time is right. The wicked will stop at nothing, even the sacrifice of innocent lives, to seize these sacred treasures for their own glory and not for the glory of God.'

'No!' cried Charlie, shrinking back. 'You've got it wrong! You've mistaken me for somebody else! I need to get home!'

'My child, my child,' murmured the abbot gently. 'Your task is not to save your mother. You have your own destiny to follow.'

'How do you know about Mother? You knew my name and then –'

'I can see into your soul, Charlie. I see that you fear for your mother, but you are far from home and you cannot help her now. But there is something you can do to help us.'

Abbot Oswald fumbled with the large gold and amber cross around his waist, releasing it from the leather thong that bound it there.

'Take this cross and wear it at all times. You will need its protection in the perilous days to come,' he insisted, pressing it into Charlie's reluctant hand.

At the abbot's firm but gentle touch, Charlie felt a delicious feeling flood through him like a warm drink on a winter's day. Abbot Oswald inclined his ear, listening to the shrieks beyond the walls of their temporary shelter.

'Embrace your fear, my child!' he said. 'Have the courage to do what is right, and fear no man. Now, take this ring from my finger. You will survive this battle but I believe that I will not.'

'Look out!' shrieked Balthazar.

Charlie spun round, screaming in terror. A bare-headed invader, hair matted with gore and blood, sprang through the flimsy doorway. Howling like a wolf, he lurched towards Charlie, brandishing his battleaxe, his face grotesquely lit by the flames from the brazier.

'Help!' shrieked Charlie, covering his head with his arms. 'Help!'

In an instant the abbot sprang forward, planting his stout body between Charlie and his attacker.

'Balthazar! Help! I don't want to die. Not here. Not like this!'

'Fly, Charlie, fly,' screamed the abbot. 'Run for your life!'

Charlie felt something land lightly on his shoulder, claws extended. 'Do as he says, Charlie,' hissed Balthazar. 'Run for that haystack over there.'

A sudden flash of lightning turned Charlie's blond hair to white flame as he streaked across the clearing, clutching the abbot's cross in his hand. He plunged head first into the hard sharp hay, burrowing down deep into the centre of the stack, ripping his skin as he scrabbled in.

'Stop trembling, Charlie,' hissed Balthazar. 'Keep still. You'll give away our hiding place.'

'They'll kill the abbot, and I didn't even take the ring,' panted Charlie in dismay.

'The Devil take the ring, Charlie – and keep that noise down if you value your life!'

Charlie lost track of how long they crouched, cowering in the haystack, listening as the cries of battle receded down towards the shoreline. He struggled stiffly up into the daylight, spitting out pieces of straw. Bloody corpses lay everywhere and the long ships had gone.

'Who were those barbarians?' asked Charlie, gazing around at the smoking ruins.

'Abbot Oswald said something about northern raiders,' said Balthazar. 'I think you'd call them Vikings.'

'Where is Abbot Oswald?' gasped Charlie. 'He wanted to give me his ring.' But Balthazar was already stalking off in the direction of the burnt-out remains of the blacksmith's hut. 'Wait, Balthazar! Let's try to find him at least,' called Charlie, stumbling to keep up. 'I'm sure he'd help us if he could.'

'Charlie!' growled Balthazar gravely.

'He thought he wasn't going to survive the battle but ...'

'And he was right!' said Balthazar grimly, crouching over a body, his hackles bristling. 'Look over here!'

Charlie knew it was the abbot even before he turned him over from where he lay face down with a long shafted axe in his back. His face was covered in sand and mud, his scant hair matted with blood.

'Abbot Oswald!' he groaned, reaching out a trembling hand to touch the lifeless face, a great sob heaving in his chest. 'Murdering barbarians! How could they do this?'

The abbot had said he was brave, but now all courage and hope had gone. Charlie knelt on the bloodstained earth and allowed the burning tears to flow down his face at last.

'At least I can take the ring for him now,' sobbed Charlie.

'You can't even do that,' spat Balthazar angrily. 'Someone's chopped his hand off!'

Only a gruesome stump remained of the hand on which Abbot Oswald had worn the carnelian ring, the blood already black around the crusted wound.

'Ugh!' cried Charlie, jumping back. 'Someone must have hacked off his hand to take the ring! Balthazar! I knew I recognized the name. Abbot Oswald. Back in the parish church at home there's a relic ... a holy hand ... it has a ring on its finger. The hand of Saint Oswald!'

Northumbria

AD 1100

18
Father Bernard

Father Bernard's study was a cosy little room tucked away at the top of a flight of stone stairs leading up from the main library. Jovial, plump and easy-going, Father Bernard, the librarian, was also head of the scriptorium, where the more learned monks would sit for hours copying out scholarly texts by hand. Marian found him peering at a ruined manuscript propped up on a sloping wooden desk, blots of crimson ink obscuring the neat black lettering. He straightened up as he heard her come in.

'I did knock, Father, but there was no reply,' she apologized, glancing suspiciously towards the stairs.

'Spoilt – quite ruined,' he murmured under his breath as he rubbed his stiff back. 'Ah, Marian, my dear. Is it time for your lesson? I was just examining the manuscript poor Brother Harold damaged the day he died. I had only just received it for our collection – all the way from Italy! So clumsy with the crimson ink, God rest his soul. Put another log on the fire if you would be so kind, and come and sit down. What is it, my dear? Why are you looking at me like that?'

'Oh … er … nothing really, Father. Just feeling a bit uneasy, you know, what with the murder and everything …' she stammered desolately. She'd been looking for Charlie all morning, but it was difficult to know where to start when someone had simply vanished before your eyes. She flung the fragrant wood on to the fire and wiped her dirty hands on her robe.

'Well now,' said Father Bernard, a deep furrow between his brows. 'What shall we do today? A little reading perhaps, or some mathematics, or maybe just a friendly chat? Perhaps you would like to tell me what you were doing hiding in the choir stalls in the middle of the night with a boy from the kitchens?'

Marian looked up, startled.

'Oh, I have eyes everywhere, my dear,' said Father Bernard severely, scratching the crisp grey curls beneath his shaven tonsure. 'What were you up to, young lady? This is a serious matter. There is evil lurking within the walls of this abbey. You must have a care who you consort with and where you go alone – treat every stranger with suspicion. What were you doing?'

Marian hesitated. Charlie had warned her to trust nobody, even people like Father Bernard. And even if she could rely on him, he'd never believe her story of a disappearing scullion. But then again, she had no other friend to confide in, and Father Bernard was staring at her sternly, intent on an answer.

'And so we thought we could try and find out what killed Brother Harold,' concluded Marian. Almost against her will, it had all come tumbling out – in a dreadful muddle. 'It seemed a good plan. Charlie's mother knows all about herbs and plants. He had lots of good ideas about how to investigate the murder. We wanted to see if we could find any books on poisoning in the library. I'm sure you'll think I'm making it all up because I don't have any friends, but honestly, I'm not. He was there one minute and gone the next!'

Father Bernard was leaning forward, earnestly studying her with a worried frown, the tips of his fingers forming a steeple under his nose.

'Tell me my dear, do you feel quite well? You never look very well, much too thin and pale, but do you feel your normal self? No pain? No fever?'

'I'm quite well, Father Bernard, in my body. I'm beginning to wonder if I'm not well in my mind.'

'Hmm. Well, the fact that you're wondering makes me think the opposite. The sick in mind rarely recognize the symptoms in themselves.' He was pacing the room now, his sandalled feet crunching on the fresh rushes. 'You are a truthful girl, I think?' He raised his bushy brows at her quizzically. 'Against my better judgement, I am inclined to believe your tale. However, my advice would be to put this young scullion out of your mind.' He smiled at her kindly. 'I think your paths are unlikely to cross again. Hmm,' he mused 'I have heard of such things. A wandering spirit unable to find rest, a lost soul perhaps.'

Marian didn't feel like arguing with Father Bernard, but Charlie had seemed solid enough to her until he disappeared, a boy of flesh and blood, not a wandering spirit. She felt wretched at the thought of never seeing him again, just as they had become friends.

'And I would advise you most strongly, my dear,' Father Bernard went on, his blue eyes grave and unsmiling, 'not to meddle in things you do not understand. There is a miscreant in this monastery who has opened his soul to the Devil. The forces of Satan throng around us. An intruder has gained access to a locked library, and an innocent novice has been murdered. These are grave matters, Marian. They are not the stuff of children's games! Leave these investigations to those equipped to deal with them.'

There was a knock on the door.

'Enter,' called Father Bernard, looking relieved.

A lanky young boy in the grey habit of a novice hovered on the threshold clutching some volumes.

'I've found those old medical books you asked me to look for, Father.'

'Ah, yes,' replied Father Bernard hastily. He immediately began ushering the boy out, glancing nervously in Marian's direction.

'I'll come with you and check them over,' he said as he bundled the boy out of the room. He popped his head back round the door, just as it was closing. 'Carry on learning those Latin prayers by heart, my dear.' He went out banging the door behind him.

Curious, thought Marian. I wasn't learning any Latin prayers. He seemed in such a hurry to get the young novice out of the way. She wandered slowly towards the door, idly picking up a volume, bound in scarlet goatskin that lay on the table. With difficulty, she spelt out the words of the title, painted in gold on the spine.

'"*Venena et purgationes*",' she read. 'I don't know about the second word, but I'm sure *venenum* means poison,' she whispered to herself in dismay. 'What could Father Bernard possibly want with this? Maybe Charlie was right after all!'

Marian felt angry with herself. Charlie had told her to trust no one, and the librarian had been acting in a most peculiar fashion. He hadn't seemed to want to discuss the matter of the murdered novice at all – certainly not with her. Could the culprit really be Father Bernard?

'It's exactly the book that Charlie wanted,' she murmured to herself, frowning. 'But what's the point of it all now?'

She sighed wearily. How could she read the book without Charlie? She hesitated for a moment, and then slipped the volume inside the lining of her cloak. Maybe a breath of sea air would clear her head. Hurriedly closing the door behind her, she tripped quietly down the stairs.

19
Black Sheep and Crows' Feathers

Marian breathed in the fresh salty air as she ambled along the cliff top, trying to order her jumbled thoughts. She felt guilty about Charlie. She'd refused to listen every time he had tried to explain where he'd come from, and yet he had vanished in front of her eyes.

The afternoon sunshine felt warm on her neck. A delicious smell of roasting meat tickled her nostrils, mingling with a sweet aroma of woodsmoke that rose from beyond the edge of the cliff. Marian peered over. The smell of food was coming from below. How odd. Surely nobody would choose to live on this desolate cliff side. Cautiously, she began to pick her way down some rough broad ledges, rather like steps, cut into the steep incline. As the smell grew stronger and more tempting, Marian noticed a narrow outcrop, which seemed to form the entrance to a cave. The mouth-watering odours were coming from inside.

The earth floor at the cave's entrance was sandy and dry.

She crept inside, holding her breath, trying not to make a sound. Gradually leaving the daylight behind, she groped around the walls towards the delicious smell. A faint glow attracted her attention followed by a thin wisp of smoke, which came spiralling through a crack in the cave wall. The outer cave seemed to lead into another chamber behind it.

A large fire blazed in the middle of the sandy floor, within a ring of stones. The appetizing smell was coming from a large plump rabbit suspended over the fire. As her eyes grew accustomed to the light, Marian could make out piles of driftwood and kindling neatly stacked against the uneven walls. An assortment of fresh fish hung from a wooden rack. And then she froze in horror, her breath catching in her throat.

The body of a double-headed lamb stood in an alcove, surrounded by a circle of black candles, its two heads staring menacingly in opposite directions. Marian's hair rose on her neck. Black sheep's fleece and crows' feathers spilled from a huge trunk open against the wall. The wool of a black sheep could steal the breath of a sleeping man, and then be used to bewitch him! And surely that was a human hand, a hand of flesh, the black skin dried and shrivelled against the bones. She had heard of such things, cut from the corpses of hanged men, objects of great magical power.

Marian fought down a scream. As she tried to retrace her steps, she stumbled against an obstacle in the gloomy shadows. It was a large basket, rather like a herb basket from the kitchen. She grabbed its handle to stop it falling over, but somebody had sharp ears. There was a dry cough.

'Who's there? Is that you, my dear?' enquired a thin reedy voice. 'It's not your usual day. Is anything amiss?'

An old man in a long rusty robe shuffled into the firelight, peering into the gloom with milky sightless eyes. He cocked his head like a crow, listening. Marian shrank back against the cave wall, the basket handle clasped in her hands, breathing as quietly as she could. The old hermit's bare feet were long and bony, his black toenails so overgrown that they curled under his feet like claws. Matted grey hair and a wild beard almost covered his face. Moving painfully, he felt his way with fragile bony arms. He cupped a gnarled old hand around his ear, straining for any sound.

'It is you, isn't it, my precious one?' he called again, anxiety in his hoarse cracked voice. 'Speak up!' His nostrils flared, sniffing the air. 'It's not you is it? You don't smell right.' His voice was threatening, with only a hint of fear. His face darkened. 'Reveal yourself, intruder! Who are you?'

Marian whimpered, cringing back, rigid with fear. Then she turned and fled down the sandy passageway between the caves, smashing her knuckles on the rough walls in her panic to reach the daylight. She could hear the soft shuffle of bare feet on the cave floor and the wheezing of the old man's laboured breathing behind her.

'A curse on you, intruder!' he screamed. 'Leave this place. May you plummet to your death! May you be dashed into a thousand pieces!'

Out in the fresh air once again, Marian sped along the narrow ledge without a thought for the treacherous drop, and up the rough steps in the granite cliff side. She bunched her trailing gown in her fist, only stopping for breath when she had left the cavern far below.

It was not until she was nearing the cliff top and safety that she realized that she was still clutching the old man's basket. It was full of apples. The afternoon sun emerged from behind a cloud, glinting on something in the bottom. She put in her hand and pushed aside the fruit. It was a bundle of carefully rolled parchment, tied together with a piece of black greasy cloth. Marian lifted the roll out carefully and slipped off the binding.

There were a number of sheets of parchment covered in neat black lettering, beautifully illustrated in the manner of the monks, with paintings all around the edges in emerald green and scarlet, sapphire blue and silver leaf. She was not a good reader, but she could spell out a few easy words.

'L … o … i … n – loin of m … u … t … mutton. Loin of Mutton with o … n … i … onion sauce. Loin of mutton with onion sauce.'

Marian felt a shiver run down her spine. She unrolled the next piece of parchment.

'R … o … a … s … t – roast hog! It's the recipes! I've found the recipes. Charlie! Where in the world are you? I've found the missing recipes!'

'Are you all right, Balthazar?' said Charlie, scrambling up from a bumpy cliff-top landing. He stared around in bewilderment, blinking stars from his eyes. 'That took me by surprise!'

'I most certainly am not all right!' growled the cat,

shaking himself down. 'Why didn't you keep your arms still? You nearly knocked me off your shoulder.'

Charlie breathed a sigh of relief to be back. His home in Essex would be preferable, but better here than where they'd just come from! He knew exactly where he was. He was in the very same place where he had found the butchered body of Abbot Oswald, but in a completely different time. The cliffs and bay were largely the same shape, but in place of the old wooden church and simple dwellings, there was now the monastery of fine red sandstone, and instead of a rough wooden fortress, there was the grim shape of Goslar Castle. The slaughtered corpses and smoking ruins had given way to a bright winter's afternoon.

'Oh, no! Look who's here,' groaned Balthazar, as Marian appeared from behind a scrubby bush, a puzzled frown on her face. 'Lady Trouble! That's all we need,' he snarled, dusting himself off grumpily. 'I'm off!'

Marian was on her way back to the castle with the recipes, wondering what to do and wishing that Charlie had been around to talk it over.

'Marian!' cried Charlie, startled.

'Charlie! I didn't see you!'

They clutched one another, both talking at once.

'What happened to you?' exclaimed Marian, touching him to check that he was real. 'Where on earth have you been? I've been looking for you everywhere. I'm so sorry I mocked you and said I didn't believe you. You just melted away under my hand in the choir stalls. I reached out to touch you and you just … just … dissolved. Look at you! You're covered in cuts.'

Charlie's head throbbed.

'I'm sorry, Marian. I'm going to have to sit down.'

He glanced wearily at the basket she had put down on the grass.

'I've got so much to tell you,' she said, following his gaze. 'I don't know where to begin.'

'I've got so much to tell you too, Marian, but first I need one of those apples.'

20
Plans in the Pigeon Loft

'Abbot Oswald wanted to give me a gold ring with a blood-red stone,' explained Charlie excitedly, flinging away his third apple core, 'and there's supposed to be a clue hidden inside it – to where some ancient monastery treasure lies hidden. He recognized me, Marian. I know it sounds far-fetched but he knew my name! He called me a "wanderer through time" and said I would be the person to restore the lost treasure to the abbey!'

'The lost treasure!' exclaimed Marian.

'You mean you know about it?' said Charlie, surprised.

'Well, yes, of course! I've known about it all my life. It's a well-known legend – a secret hoard of treasure, hidden at the time of the Viking raids, about … oh, I'm no good at dates … about three hundred years ago. So where is this ring? Let me see it.'

'That's the problem,' groaned Charlie. 'I haven't brought it. He was just about to give it to me when I was set upon by a Viking warrior. The abbot saved my life. He put himself between me and my attacker.'

'Was he killed?' asked Marian in dismay.

'He didn't stand a chance,' said Charlie bitterly. 'I found his mangled corpse the next morning. It was gruesome … and he'd so much wanted me to take the ring.'

'So why didn't you take it from the body?' asked Marian. 'It wouldn't have been stealing. He'd already told you he wanted …'

'It was too late, Marian. When I bent down to look for the ring on his hand … I … I … it's too horrible … there was just a bloody stump. His hand had been cut off at the wrist.'

Marian caught her breath. 'The Hand of Saint Oswald!' she gasped. 'It must be! A red stone did you say, in a gold setting? The hand is the abbey's most sacred relic. They keep it in the church. There's a shrine to him – Saint Oswald, I mean. The hand has healing powers.'

'The hand of Saint Oswald is in the abbey?' said Charlie incredulously.

'Oh, yes. The holiest saint that ever lived!'

'But there's a relic of Saint Oswald's hand back in my church at home. And there's a ring on its finger!'

'You've seen a vision of Saint Oswald, Charlie. Pilgrims come for miles to see what you've seen.'

'It wasn't a vision, Marian. You don't understand. I actually saw him in the flesh! I spoke with him.' Charlie kicked at a piece of turf with his foot. 'You don't believe me, do you?'

Marian looked at him doubtfully.

'Why should you believe me?' said Charlie. 'It's hard to understand myself. I came here from another time and ... and now I've been back to Abbot Oswald's time, and all I really want to do is to go home.'

'I wouldn't have believed you except that ... when you disappeared in the church you simply melted under my hand. I thought you were making up tales before, and then you vanished in front of me! I have to believe you after all that. And then there's the lost monastery treasure part – it's a legend everyone knows.' She paused. 'Of course I believe you. Now, what else did Saint Oswald say to you?'

'It's not that easy to remember,' said Charlie, looking worried. 'There was a battle going on outside. People were being hideously slaughtered. We were hiding in this blacksmith's hut and then I was attacked.'

'You must think, Charlie! Every single word might be important!'

Charlie closed his eyes, desperately trying to recall every one of the old monk's words.

'He said I had to use the secret that the ring contained with wisdom and that I'd know when the time was right. He said wicked people were prepared to sacrifice innocent lives to get hold of the treasure for their own glory.'

'Innocent lives? Do you think he meant that people would be prepared to kill for it?' asked Marian, alarmed.

'I suppose so – what else could it mean? Oh, yes, and he also gave me this,' he added. Charlie dug in his cloak pocket and held out the amber cross. 'He said something really strange about this too – told me to wear it at all times and that I would need its protection in the perilous days to come.'

Marian fingered the golden stone, frowning. 'That's worrying, Charlie. All this talk about sacrificing innocent lives is making me nervous – you know, what with the murder of poor Brother Harold and everything. Our days are perilous enough already.'

Charlie looked startled. 'Marian! You don't think Brother Harold's death could have anything to do with the lost monastery treasure, do you? I mean, we were on a quest to try to find a book on poisoning in the library when I, well, you know …'

'When you disappeared, you mean?' finished Marian, looking doubtful. 'But what can missing recipes and the abbey's long-lost treasure possibly have in common?'

'It just seems rather odd, that's all – finding out about the ring at just that moment. Almost as if there's a purpose behind everything. That's another thing Saint Oswald said to me – there's a purpose to everything and as I grew in wisdom I would understand.' He shrugged. 'Anyway, enough of me. You said you'd got something to tell,' said Charlie.

'Yes, I have. You're not the only one who has adventures, you know. You'll never believe what I've found – at the bottom of this basket of apples!'

She produced the pages of parchment with a flourish, handing them to Charlie.

'"Loin of Mutton with onion sauce"?' he read. 'What on earth … are these the recipes? I can't believe it, Marian – the missing recipes! Where on earth did you find them?' he cried, grabbing her by the shoulders. 'Brilliant! You're a marvel.'

'You've not done so badly yourself,' grinned Marian.

By the time Marian had finished telling Charlie about her encounter with the hermit, the sun was going down.

'He sounds absolutely terrifying!' said Charlie. 'So you think the old hermit stole the recipes from the Book?'

'Oh, heavens no! He's just a scary old man – absolutely ancient I should say. I can't think what they were doing there though. You should have seen the things he had in his lair, Charlie – black candles, black sheep's wool ...'

Charlie grimaced. 'There's so much to work out. First of all, who is drugging novices in order to steal recipes? Don't forget, Marian, that person is now a murderer –'

'Yes,' interrupted Marian, 'and why are they doing it? If we knew why, it would help us work out who it could be.'

'That's right,' agreed Charlie. 'By the way – you didn't get a chance to look in the library the night I disappeared, I suppose?'

'No. I was so shocked when you vanished that I just went back to my room in the castle. But I have managed to borrow a book that might be about poisoning. I'm not absolutely sure about the title – it's in Latin.'

'Well, that's a good start! See if you can get it to me as soon as possible. And let's try and have a look at Saint Oswald's hand in the chapel as well. See if there's anything in the ring. Saint Oswald told me it contained a secret that I must use when the time is right. I ought at least to try and find out what it is.'

'I wonder if there's any other way into the chapel apart from through the main door. I don't fancy sneaking in before matins again,' said Marian.

'Find out and get a message to me. Oh, Marian, if only you could have seen Saint Oswald. He was so … well … well … holy.' Charlie looked embarrassed.

'I do believe you, Charlie,' said Marian reassuringly. 'It's an amazing story. Wouldn't it be wonderful if we found the ancient monastery's missing treasure? I'm sorry I made fun of you before, about your shoes and things and the way you speak. And … and I'm truly sorry about your mother.'

Charlie smiled sadly. 'I forgive you, Marian. It's not exactly a likely story. Look– the sun's going down. I'd better get back to the kitchens. Goodness knows how I'll explain where I've been!'

'You'll think of something. Here – take this.'

Marian thrust the basket of apples into Charlie's hands. 'This looks as if it comes from the kitchens. You look after the recipes, Charlie. Hide them under your mattress or something, but don't lose them. And Charlie,' she pleaded, 'don't go disappearing again!'

The next day dragged past while Charlie waited impatiently for news from Marian. He was in the pigeon loft with Eadgyth when Marian finally caught up with him. Eadgyth was choosing a few young fat ones for Lady Goslar's dinner.

The pigeon loft was a tall circular building with nesting boxes running from floor to ceiling. The floor and walls were white with pigeon droppings. Eadgyth was precariously perched at the top of a groaning ladder, her neat little feet balanced on a rung. She was leaning right into a nesting box, her enormous bottom sticking out.

'Hurry up, Eadgyth!' choked Charlie. 'I can't breathe in here. There isn't that much difference between them, surely. They all look pretty fat to me.'

'I don't know how you have the cheek to moan!' she snapped, struggling with a bird. 'You still haven't explained what you were up to yesterday when you was needed for stuffing hog's bladders! Sturgeon don't take kindly to scullions skiving off and no more do I! Now, shurrup and push me along again. Here – catch!' She tossed down two plump pigeons, their necks freshly wrung.

'Well done, Charlie! Don't drop them now. It damages the delicate flesh.'

Marian was lurking in the doorway. She thought she'd never attract his attention above the noise of cooing birds and flapping wings. She threw a smooth stone, catching Charlie neatly between the shoulder blades. He tiptoed towards the door.

'I can't be long,' he whispered, glancing behind him.

'Tonight,' she hissed. 'Meet me at the church at midnight – west side. I've found a way in.'

'I've finished now, Charlie,' trilled Eadgyth merrily as Charlie scuttled back to catch the last two pigeons. 'Steady the ladder now. I'm coming down!'

21
The Carnelian Ring

Charlie kept well into the shadows. The moon was full and the clear sky was pricked with stars, a sprinkling of frost on the ground. The gloomy castle hunched behind him, silent and brooding. He clutched his cloak around him, but it wasn't only the biting cold that made him shiver. What on earth was he doing out here in the middle of the night with a murderer about? Saint Oswald's golden cross lay warm on his chest on its leather thong, tucked beneath his clothes. As he skirted the shadowy church, he heard a voice. 'Here, over here,' it hissed.

Charlie jumped, his nerves raw. 'It's only Marian,' he scolded himself. Glancing behind, he moved quickly in the direction of her voice. It was coming from behind a grating set in the lower part of the church wall.

'I'm down here,' she whispered. 'See those steps outside leading below ground level? Come down those and I'll open the door.'

Charlie picked his way carefully down the slippery steps. He heard the rusty grate of heavy iron bolts and the groan of hinges as the door opened inwards to reveal Marian, holding a black lantern.

'Didn't want you to get covered in scalding wax like last time,' she said mischievously.

'What are we doing down here?' said Charlie, squinting into the darkness.

'We're in the catacombs under the church,' said Marian. 'Listen! We can get up into the church from here. We've got a couple of hours before matins, so we should be able to get a look at the hand and back down again before the monks arrive. Follow me.'

They crept down into the huge echoing cavern beneath the church. It was noisy after the silence outside: rats scurrying and the musical plopping of water dropping into puddles on the flagged stone floor. Marian shrank away as they skirted the tombs and stone coffins.

'Ugh!' she groaned, clutching Charlie's arm, her thin fingers digging into his flesh. The light from her lantern pooled around them, falling on piles of bones that lay in niches, pyramids of neatly stacked skulls, grinning against the dripping walls. She felt her knees about to give way. 'I ... I ... didn't think it would be like this. J ... just imagine all the tombs opening up and the skeletons rising out of them!'

Charlie laughed uneasily, his fingers locking around Marian's. Her skin felt clammy. An unearthly coldness crept up through the floor.

'Look,' said Marian, holding up the trembling lantern,

'here's a flight of stairs. It must lead up into the nave of the church.'

'Come on then! What are we waiting for?' gulped Charlie, breathing deeply to calm himself. 'We haven't got all night.'

'I've just got cold feet, that's all,' said Marian, pulling back.

'So have I,' said Charlie firmly, 'and they won't get any warmer by standing here – so come on.'

The shrine of Saint Oswald was in a tiny side chapel. Pale-silver moonlight streamed through an arched window, dappling the face of the stone abbot as it lay on top of the granite tomb. His arms were crossed over his chest, and where the missing hand should have been there was only a stump, the hand missing from the wrist down. The flanks of the tomb were covered with carvings of scenes from Saint Oswald's life – the saint curing the sick and working miracles. Around the walls of the little chapel were crutches, walking sticks and bits of old cloth that looked like discarded bandages.

'There's a day in summer,' whispered Marian, 'when cripples come here to touch the holy hand. If there's a miracle, they leave their crutches here.'

Charlie nodded distractedly. Something odd was happening to Saint Oswald's golden cross. It was heating up on his chest, getting warmer by the second.

'This is the tomb,' said Marian, 'but where's the hand?'

Charlie knew already. 'It's behind the tomb – in a niche at the back.'

'But how do you know?'

Charlie didn't answer. His fingers crept along the smooth stone. 'Here it is,' he whispered.

The golden casket gleamed in the flickering lantern light. Charlie delicately pulled aside the scarlet silk to reveal the skeletal hand, white and fleshless, the huge carnelian ring glowing on its finger. He felt a shudder pass through his body.

'Ugh! It's revolting!' said Marian. 'What's the matter, Charlie?' She clutched his sleeve in alarm. She had a sudden ghastly vision of him disappearing again.

Charlie was gripping the burning cross around his neck, tears pricking his eyes.

'It is the same hand, Marian,' he said softly, 'the one in the church at home – the same casket, everything!'

'Come on, Charlie,' said Marian impatiently. 'We'd better take a look at the ring.' She was keen to get away. 'Can you see how to open it?'

'I think you have to slide your thumbnail around the stone to spring a trap. Go on, you do it, Marian, my hands are shaking.'

At first nothing happened. She tried again, pressing harder. There was a faint pinging sound as the stone shot up to reveal a cavity deep within the setting. With trembling hand, Marian tipped the ring sideways. Her heart gave a jolt as a small piece of yellow parchment dropped into her palm.

'So it is true, Charlie!'

Charlie swallowed. 'I never doubted it for a moment,' he said solemnly.

'Come on then,' breathed Marian. 'Let's put the ring back and get out of here.'

Charlie carefully replaced the ring on the finger, folding the soft cloth back over the hand.

'Hurry up, Charlie,' hissed Marian. 'We've got what we came for!'

Neither of them spoke as they crept silently back down the shadowy nave to the top of the stairs leading down to the catacombs.

'Have you put the parchment somewhere safe?' Charlie whispered as they reached the bottom of the stone staircase.

'In my pocket,' said Marian in a small voice, holding up the lantern. 'I wish there was another way out, Charlie. I can't face going back through these tombs again.'

Somewhere in the distance, a door blew shut with a bang.

'W … what on earth …?' cried Marian.

'I … I can't have shut it properly when we came in,' stammered Charlie shakily. 'It … it must be the wind …'

An icy blast of cold air sliced through the vault. The lantern flared crazily and then went out.

'Heeeelp!' screamed Marian, her nerve finally giving way. She plunged blindly into the darkness, clawing past the tombs. Charlie could hear her fearful whimpers as she stumbled on the uneven floor.

'Wait, Marian! Come back!' he yelled, charging after her, narrowly avoiding a pile of leering skulls. They wobbled drunkenly as the tail of his cloak caught the edge of the pile. 'How can we be sure it was the wind …?'

Outside in the cold full moon they leaned panting against the church wall.

'I'm sorry,' said Marian, a little shamefaced. 'When the lantern blew out I lost my head!'

'I'm sure I shut the door behind me when I came in.' Charlie looked scared. 'What do we do now?'

'Come back to my room and we'll look at the parchment,' said Marian. 'I'm chilled to the bone.'

They left the shadow of the church and began to scramble through the bushes towards the garden. Just as they emerged, Charlie stepped back suddenly, treading hard on Marian's foot.

'Ouch! Mind where you're –'

'Shh. There's someone there,' warned Charlie.

'Maybe it's the murderer,' gasped Marian, clutching his cloak. 'Oh, God, I don't think I can stand much more of this.'

Charlie silently pressed aside some branches and peered through. A large figure crouched near the herb beds in the shadow of the garden wall, rummaging around in the earth as if searching for something.

'Doesn't look like a murderer,' hissed Charlie. 'He's collecting something and filling his basket. It's a funny time to be out in the garden.'

'It looks like a woman,' said Marian.

As if it felt it was being watched, the figure turned abruptly and stared hard into the bushes. Marian and Charlie fled, struggling back through the shrubbery, fighting with their cloaks as they caught on the undergrowth, round the gloomy church and through the graveyard.

'Wait for me, Marian!' called Charlie. 'I can't run in this cloak. Wait!'

Marian darted out of sight behind a yew tree in the middle of the graveyard. A moment later, Charlie heard a scream that turned his blood to ice.

22
The Screaming Mandrake

'Charlie, Charlie, help!' screamed Marian. 'Help me somebody, please!'

Blood-curdling sounds were coming from the other side of the graveyard's low wall. Charlie pelted across the churchyard to where Marian lay writhing on the ground, tugging wildly at a root that had coiled itself around her ankle.

'Get this thing off me! Get it off! It's alive!'

In an instant Charlie was down on his knees by Marian's side, fighting with the thick fleshy plant with his bare hands. A deerhound was tied to the same root by a rope wound tightly around its neck. It lay whimpering on its side next to Marian, its mouth hanging open, tongue lolling from foam-flecked jaws.

'Ugh! What is it, Charlie? Can you get me free?' cried Marian, her eyes wide with terror.

'Mandrake,' panted Charlie, almost sobbing from the effort of battling with the plant. 'It's deadly stuff! Especially when it's still in the ground.'

No sooner had he freed Marian's foot than another tendril snaked around her leg again. A sickening fetid odour hung all around. The plant had been wrenched half out of the ground. It lay shrieking by her side, its berries glowing with a cold pale light. Summoning all his strength, Charlie forced the twisted root apart. He released Marian's foot and leapt swiftly aside before it had a chance to wind itself around him.

'Run, Marian!' he cried desperately.

'I can't! I've sprained my ankle,' she wailed.

'You must! Do what I tell you. Its scream alone can kill! I'll bring the dog,' he yelled, fumbling to undo the cord that bound the animal to the plant. 'Run, Marian! Run!'

'I've never been so terrified in all my life,' moaned Marian, clutching her swollen ankle in front of the fire in her turret room.

'You've had a lucky escape – and so did the poor dog. A few more minutes and he'd have pulled up the entire root, and that would have been the end of him, poor fellow.'

Charlie was sitting on Marian's bed, nursing the dog's grey head in his lap.

'It's Otto, Eadgyth's dog. He lives in the kitchens,' said Charlie.

'Is he going to be all right?' Marian was in tears. 'What was that spine-chilling screaming – and the smell? I can't get it out of my nostrils.'

'It's called the screaming mandrake. It screams horribly when anyone tries to pick it. It's a powerful poison. That's why Otto was there.'

'Otto?'

'Mandrake's used by people who dabble in black magic. They use dogs to pull it up for them – the dogs usually die in the attempt. It's easy to find because the berries glow in the dark and it gives off that revolting smell.'

'So somebody's trying to gather mandrake,' said Marian in a horrified voice, 'and they were using poor Otto to do the dangerous part?'

'I've got a horrible feeling about all this,' said Charlie. 'There's something really evil going on. There's been a murder, Marian, and we think the victim was poisoned, and now we've found Otto tied to the wailing mandrake.'

'Talking of murders, here's the book I borrowed from Father Bernard.'

'"*Venena et purgationes*",' read Charlie, stroking the scarlet spine. '*Poisons and Purges*! Wonderful!'

Marian looked pleased. 'I wonder what he was doing with it,' she frowned.

Charlie raised an eyebrow.

'I know,' she muttered. 'Trust nobody! But I just don't want to suspect the Fathers.'

Charlie took the book from Marian. 'Everyone's a suspect, especially those with obvious motives, Marian!'

'What do you mean?' she said sharply.

'Oh, just something I've been mulling over since my meeting with Saint Oswald. If these mysteries are linked somehow – you know, the treasure and the murder – then Father Bernard could have as good a motive to be after the treasure as anyone. You told me yourself he likes to collect valuable ancient manuscripts. Well, that all costs money.'

'Abbot Gregory wants to rebuild the bell tower and Father Simeon wants to extend the infirmary.'

'Like I said, trust no one,' said Charlie, opening the book. 'Now, this is exactly the volume I need to look up the novices' symptoms. Can I take it until tomorrow?' he said, leafing through. 'Ah, here's mandrake. There's even a drawing.'

'How odd,' said Marian, peering at the spidery picture. 'That strange forked root looks like a little wizened person with legs.'

'And the wispy top looks like hair,' said Charlie.

'You know, I feel as if I've seen something like this before,' said Marian, biting her nail.

'Hadn't we better look at the parchment from Saint Oswald's ring?' said Charlie, closing the book. 'So much has happened we're forgetting what we went to the chapel for in the first place.'

Marian placed the fragile parchment on a low wooden table.

'Oh, no!' groaned Charlie.

'What's the matter?' asked Marian, leaning over his shoulder.

'I thought it was too good to be true. It's written in Saxon runes, and I don't know the runic alphabet! I can read Latin, but not this,' sighed Charlie. 'I hoped there'd be something else to help us – like a map.'

'I expect Father Bernard could read it,' said Marian, 'except I don't want him to know anything about us meddling with the relic. He'd be so angry.'

Charlie looked thoughtful. 'I don't want to tell Father

Bernard too much, Marian. Could you copy it out on to some fresh parchment and ask him? He doesn't have to know where it came from. You know, Marian, I have such a weird feeling about this ring. I've looked at it so many times in the church at home, and then I go back to Viking times and Saint Oswald tries to give it to me, and now it turns up here in the abbey at Goslar Castle. It's as if it were following me around … or me it!'

'I can give Father Bernard the riddle in the morning,' said Marian, 'but I won't say anything about where I found it.'

Charlie looked sceptical.

'Well, how else can we find out what it says?' urged Marian.

'I suppose so, but not a word about where it came from. Promise me?'

Marian nodded solemnly.

'Look, I'd better be going,' said Charlie. 'There's nothing more we can do tonight. Look after Otto. Keep him warm and give him something to drink if he wakes up,' said Charlie, a little downcast. He was reluctant to leave Marian's comfortable room.

'Cheer up, Charlie. At least we found the ring and it did have something in it. We must make a better plan to meet this time. How about the herb garden tomorrow morning? I'm having a lute lesson. Will that give you long enough to look at the book?'

'Yes. I'll see what I can manage, but I can't always get away just when it suits me.' He flung the cloak around his shoulders. 'I'll be off then,' said Charlie, more cheerfully than he felt.

He was just opening the door to leave when Marian suddenly caught her breath.

'What?' said Charlie.

'I've remembered where I've seen the mandrake root before. It was in that old hermit's cave! I didn't know what they were – all hanging up in a line, like tiny little corpses.'

Charlie sneaked across the kitchen yard, clutching the book under his cloak. He crept over to his straw pallet, checking for the hidden herbal with the recipes tucked inside it. He cast a wary glance over the slumbering bodies in the kitchen before he drew out the book. *Poisons and Purges.* Just the thing!

He strained his eyes in the dim firelight, trying to translate the close-written Latin text. He knew exactly what he was looking for – some kind of poisonous plant which caused drowsiness, fever, stomach cramps and a feeling of numbness.

Charlie felt a familiar tickle on his cheekbone.

'Balthazar! Thank heavens. You're here one minute, gone the next. What are you up to now?'

'Ssh! Keep your voice down.'

'Where have you been?' whispered Charlie. 'I've just had the most horrible experience with a mandrake root!'

'Yes I know all about it. You went and rescued that infernal cat chaser. Honestly Charlie, I could scratch you to pieces!'

'How do you know, Balthazar?'

'I was behind you all the time. Oh, and by the way,' he added airily, 'your mother could read runes!'

Balthazar leapt lightly down from a barrel and began tracing shapes in the sawdust with his paw.

'There you are,' said Balthazar smugly. 'Your mother taught me how to write this. It's all I know I'm afraid, but it might help.'

Charlie peered at the pattern of straight lines in the dust. 'What's that supposed to mean?'

'It's runes, stupid. I'll read it to you. "Balthazar Ferret is a very handsome cat",' he said, flicking his whiskers. 'And by the way, you ought to be a bit more careful. You were seen sneaking out of the kitchen and coming back in just now.'

'What do you mean?' said Charlie, startled.

Balthazar nodded towards Erik's hunched form, sleeping on his pallet.

'You be careful, that's all,' he warned. 'Keep your eyes open and trust no one.'

'Are these the only symbols you know, Balthazar?' said Charlie, frowning at the dust, but there was no reply. The cat had gone.

Charlie had nothing to write with. He wanted to scribble down the pattern Balthazar had traced, before it was scuffed away.

'I know – blood writing!'

He took a piece of sharp straw from his mattress and carefully picked off a scab. He winced in pain. It had better be worth it, he thought, wiping his smarting arm on his tunic. There were plenty of letters in the message; certainly enough to make a start on decoding the riddle. Thank heavens Marian wouldn't need to bother Father Bernard about it now.

It took him quite some time to inscribe the runes into the back of his mother's herbal, but at last he turned to the book.

'Now, let's see,' muttered Charlie to himself, scanning the page. 'Figs, foxgloves and fungi. Aha, this is interesting! *Amanita phalloides* – the death cap.' Charlie translated quickly.

> The appearance resembles the edible field mushroom. Cap is a yellow-olive colour, but the gills are white. Symptoms of poisoning: stomach cramps, drowsiness, visions, delirium, fever. Numbness in the hands and feet – very common. These fungi are at their most poisonous when the moon is full.

Charlie's heart was beating fast. Toadstools! So simple. Why hadn't he guessed before? He was just on the point of closing the book when his attention was caught by two words – Holy Fire. He began translating again rapidly.

> Intensely itchy inflammation of the skin, known to drive the sufferer insane, hence the name Holy Fire – linked to a deadly fungus found in mouldy rye – intense stomach pain, vomiting – poisoning almost always results in death.

'The itching!' gasped Charlie. 'Wasn't Brother Harold driven insane by an itchy rash?'

23
Goose Eggs

'Get up, you lazy lout!' screamed Sturgeon the next morning, ripping off Charlie's cloak and flinging a tankard of icy water full in his face. Charlie struggled up, spluttering.

'What's the matter with you? Been up all night? You have to work to earn your keep in my kitchen. You're on birthday-cake duty with that lump of lard Eadgyth, and don't go helping yourself to the cream. The last scullion that tried that trick ended up baked in the cake! It's all hands to the spits today for her Ladyship's birthday, and we don't need no shirkers.'

Charlie scuttled off in search of Eadgyth, who was already scarlet in the face and removing her first batch of fig pastries from of the oven.

'Have a piece of pine-nut candy, Charlie,' she bustled, nodding towards a huge platter of sweetmeats. 'There's plenty for everyone. Now, we've got an enormous cake to bake today for that fat woman's birthday – so let's get started. Can you go down to the fowl house and get me thirty-five goose eggs? Take one of them large baskets.'

Charlie brightened. Just the chance he needed. If he was quick about collecting the eggs, he might manage to slip into the monastery garden for a minute or two.

'Thirty-five goose eggs?' queried Charlie.

'Yes, my duck. Nothing better than goose eggs for a fluffy sponge.'

* * * * *

'All right, all right, I'm going!' Charlie emerged in a storm of feathers. 'Oops!' He skidded on a large green patch of goose droppings and by some miracle managed to land on his bottom with the basket clutched firmly in both hands, all eggs intact. The furious birds loomed over him, necks poked forward, hissing angrily.

'Keep your stupid eggs then!' He'd collected thirty. 'I'll tell her that's all there were,' he muttered, scrambling to his feet and staring in dismay at his clothes. 'I look as if I've been on latrine duty, and now I've got to go and find Marian.'

He could hear the rumpus from outside the walled garden. Poor Father Patrick, thought Charlie gazing up at the music-room window.

'Splash!'

Something landed on the smooth surface of the fountain pool.

'Oh, nooo! Not my new manuscript! Marian! You little vixen. I've only just copied it out – the ink is scarcely dry.'

Marian's dismayed face appeared at the window.

'I'm sorry, Father Patrick. I didn't mean … I didn't realize … I just lost my temper,' she wailed. 'Oh dear, I can't see it anywhere. Wait – I'll go down.'

Father Patrick peered out short-sightedly. 'It's ruined. Ruined! My finest work, composed for your mother's birthday too! You wicked, wicked girl,' sobbed the music master, dabbing at his dripping nose with the sleeve of his habit. 'You've gone too far this time. Your own lute is one thing, but my original work is quite another!'

There was the sound of scurrying feet on the stairs and Marian burst into the garden, casting desperately around for the manuscript.

'Well, that was a stroke of luck anyway,' grinned Charlie. 'I wanted a word with you.' She skidded to a halt. 'Is this what you're looking for?' He held up a dripping book of music, the pages already swollen with pond water.

'Hello Charlie. Ugh! You're filthy,' she said, stepping away from him. 'What's that all over your clothes?'

'Oh, just a little bit of goose dung!'

'Poor Father Patrick,' groaned Marian, taking the sopping music book from Charlie's hands. 'I didn't mean it to land in the fountain.'

'Look, Marian,' said Charlie impatiently. 'I've found something out about the symptoms. I think it's toadstool poisoning – sounds like the death cap. They're very poisonous – can be deadly! They cause all the right kind of symptoms – drowsiness, stomach cramps, numbness. But that's not the best bit. I've even found a poison that gives its victim an itchy rash! It's a really vicious one!'

'What is it?'

'Mouldy rye! I don't know where it gets us but … and another thing. I know some runic letters so don't go asking Father Bernard about the riddle.'

Marian looked crestfallen.

'I already have!' she said glumly. 'I saw him on my way to my music lesson and I had the copy of the riddle I'd made in my pocket.'

'Oh, Marian! You didn't tell him where you got it from did you?'

'Of course not! We agreed we wouldn't, didn't we? I'm sorry, Charlie, but how was I to know you'd find out how to read runes overnight? How did you, by the way?'

'Oh, I …' he hesitated. He did trust Marian, even thought of her as a friend, but he was still reluctant to tell her about Balthazar. Better leave familiars out of it for the moment.

'Oh, I just found some letters scribbled in the back of my mother's herbal,' he said breezily. 'She knew runes, you know.'

'Did she?' said Marian, looking surprised. 'Funny you didn't say so before. I'm sorry I showed the runes to Father Bernard, but at least I've still got the parchment we found.'

She rummaged in her gown and pulled out a yellow silk purse.

'Here, you take it and see what you can make of the writing. Hey, look.' She stooped down and picked up a piece of muddy blue ribbon. 'What's this?'

Charlie didn't reply. He was crouching over the herb bed. He looked up at her, a startled expression on his face.

'I can't be certain,' he frowned, 'but I think this is a clump of *amanita phalloides*.'

'What?'

'The death cap toadstool – the one I read about. And last night was a full moon! Someone was out here last night – we saw them. They weren't just after mandrake. See these ragged stalks? Someone's been collecting toadstools!'

'Are you sure these are amanti whatnots?' asked Marian.

'I can take some back to the kitchens to check.'

Charlie gently plucked a few of the death cap toadstools and placed them on top of the pile of goose eggs in the basket.

'I must remember to wash my hands. I've got to hurry now. I'm helping with your mother's birthday cake today – that's what the eggs are for. You do realize what this means, don't you Marian? Somebody was out here picking poisonous toadstools by full moon last night, and tonight will be the night after. On six of the occasions when the novices were found drugged, there had been a full moon the night before!'

'So you think there'll be another recipe taken tonight – another novice in danger?'

'I think it's very likely! You're going to have to keep a watch on the library somehow. See if you notice anything strange.'

'Me?' exclaimed Marian.

'Well, of course you! It's Lady Goslar's birthday feast. There's no way I'll be able to get away. It's all hands to the spits in the kitchens on feast nights,' explained Charlie, echoing Sturgeon's words. 'There's no way I won't be missed. You'll have to do some snooping on your own this time!'

'But –'

'Don't look so downcast,' encouraged Charlie. 'You said you wanted an adventure. Nobody will miss you at the feast. You must do it, Marian!'

'Lady Marian!' called Father Patrick from the music-room window. 'You'll catch cold wandering around out there. Come up and make friends, Marian dear. All is forgiven. I can write my composition out again. I can remember every glorious note.'

Marian grinned. 'He always comes round in the end, poor thing. I'd better go and patch things up. I'm fond of the silly old fool really.'

'So will you do it, Marian? Stop changing the subject.'

'I'll think about it,' said Marian edgily.

Charlie looked doubtful.

'I said I'll think about it, didn't I?' she hissed savagely.

Charlie scowled and turned his back on her, walking off towards the arched entrance. Marian stood staring after him, a thin figure in his scullion's outfit, lurching awkwardly under the weight of the great kitchen basket, full of goose eggs and poisonous toadstools.

24
Secrets of the Spice Cupboard

Father Bernard jiggled the smoking logs in the stone hearth with an iron poker and then walked stiffly over to the window to stare out at the sullen grey day. The sun shone weakly, a milk-white disc in the sky, ragged clouds like smoke drifting across its face. There was a cough outside the door and a novice staggered into the room carrying a large wooden bowl of steaming water.

'Just put it down in front of the fire please, my child,' said Father Bernard gratefully.

'I put in some hog's marrow like you said, Father. I'm not sure it's the best thing though. My old grandmother always said worms were good for the rheumatics.'

'Ahem. No need to trouble yourself with worms, dear boy. This will do nicely for now.'

Father Bernard sank heavily into a low oak chair set before the fire and took off his leather boots. The warm water felt delicious and soothing around his aching toes. He'd just had a meeting with Abbot Gregory. They had agreed to put two novices on Book duty tonight instead of the customary one, and Father Bernard had volunteered to keep a watch on the library after he had locked the novices in.

'Be a good fellow and light some oil lamps for me, please. And could you pull up that small table and put it here, and pass me some fresh parchment and a quill?'

The novice began to drag the table over the rushes towards the fire.

'Not worried about tonight, my child?' enquired Father Bernard anxiously.

'Not me, Father. We've all got to take our turn on Book duty, we novices.'

'Good. Just keep your eyes and ears open, there's a good lad – there'll be another novice with you, so you can look after each other. Run along now.'

Father Bernard rummaged in the pocket of his habit for the piece of parchment Marian had given him earlier this morning. What could it possibly be? He hadn't read runes for years, but that didn't bother a scholar like Father Bernard. He soon forgot his aching feet and began to scribble, scratching rapidly with his newly sharpened quill.

'It's a riddle, I think,' he muttered to himself eagerly. 'What fun!'

Father Bernard hardly noticed that he had been sitting for some time with his feet in a bowl of cold water. The floor around him was littered with screwed-up pieces of parchment full of blots and crossings-out, but in front of him on the table lay the translation. Father Bernard's face wore a worried frown. Now, where in the world could Marian have got hold of this? He began to read aloud.

I am a tutor not in human form,
Though wrought by man and made of skin, was not of woman born,
Though leaves I have, I am yet not a tree,
Though pages serve, yet no man kneels to me.
Delve deep within my leafy heart and I'll reveal to thee,
The secrets traced upon my skin – a tasty alchemy.
I came from the dark earth and there I shall remain
Though many a sun will set and new moons wax and wane,
Until the song of birds I will enjoy again.
My whereabouts a letter doth conceal,
Which, eaten will provide a tasty meal.

Father Bernard bit the end of his quill. Most intriguing. Now, where did that young minx get such an elaborate riddle from, and what could it mean?

Charlie stepped carefully along the slippery path back to the kitchens, terrified of losing his balance on the ice. As he pushed open the kitchen door with his bottom, Eadgyth came rushing up to grab the basket.

'I'll take it. It's too heavy for you,' he said quickly, thinking of the toadstools. 'Where do you want it?'

He turned so that his body was between Eadgyth and the

basket and hastily palmed the toadstools, shaking them up the loose sleeve of his tunic.

'Just going to blow my nose, Eadgyth,' he called, walking casually towards the little nook where his straw pallet lay. He emptied the toadstools out of his sleeve and pushed them under his cloak until he could examine them more closely.

'Well done! You're starting to use that small brain of yours at last,' growled Balthazar, stepping delicately between Charlie's sleeping pallet and a barrel of salted fish.

'What do you mean?' asked Charlie, scowling. 'I haven't time to stand around chatting. I'm helping Eadgyth with the birthday cake.'

'I mean that you've brought back some toadstools. I'm impressed. If you find me the page in *Poisons and Purges* I'll do some research for you. See if your specimens match the drawings.'

Balthazar leapt neatly up on to Charlie's cloak, turning around a few times to arrange himself comfortably.

'What's this?' he asked, nudging the dirty blue ribbon with his paw.

'Marian picked it up in the garden just now. It was lying in the patch of toadstools,' he said hurriedly. 'I must get on now or Eadgyth will be fretting.'

Balthazar didn't look up. He was engrossed in the tiny print, his paw daintily holding open the page that Charlie had found for him. Charlie hurried back to Eadgyth who was already busy cracking eggs.

'How's that cream going, boys?' asked Eadgyth.

Two sweaty scullions were labouring over a huge vat of cream with whisks made of dried twigs.

'It'll never thicken, Eadgyth,' puffed one, wiping the perspiration from his brow. 'We've been whisking for half an hour already.'

'Then whisk some more, boys, and stop moaning,' she snapped impatiently. 'Now, Charlie, my love,' she said, delving in her apron for a key, 'I want you to go to Sturgeon's spice room. Don't let him catch you – he's that mean with them precious spices. Now, let's see, I need nutmeg, ginger, saffron, dates and currants … er, what else … some mace, ground cloves … ooh, and an onion.'

'An onion?' Charlie raised an eyebrow.

'Not for the cake, my duck,' she laughed.

Charlie lifted the latch to the storeroom, unprepared for the heady gush of exotic smells. Jars and bottles crowded the shelves, each carefully labelled in tiny brown writing: dried dandelion leaves, saffron, cinnamon sticks, liquorice root. Huge oak barrels split in half were piled with dried fruits, dates, raisins, figs and prunes.

'That was careless, Charlie!' growled Balthazar, squeezing in beside him.

'Gosh, Balthazar!' gasped Charlie. 'You made me jump. I thought you were researching toadstools.'

'You left one in the basket of eggs, you fool! Eadgyth found it! She seemed a bit annoyed, I don't know why.'

'Look, Balthazar, give me a hand here. I've got a long list. Can you find me an onion?'

Balthazar sprang on to a shelf and began to rummage among some ropes of garlic with his paw while Charlie scanned the shelves for spices.

'Now, just look what we have here!' hissed Balthazar triumphantly. 'You were right, Charlie! Those toadstools are poisonous. I found them in the book – and look over here!'

Behind some dried mushrooms, Charlie could just see something creamy pale and pinkish. He pushed the other string aside and groped behind them, plucking off the bottom toadstool on the cord that hung at the back. It felt spongy under his fingers, smelling of wet earth and leaf mould – and it was still damp, as if it hadn't had time to dry out. He stifled a gasp! It was only slightly duller and greyer than the specimens he had picked this morning!

'It's the same as the one I brought in just now, Balthazar. The death cap – *amanita phalloides*. In Sturgeon's spice room.'

'Yes, Charlie. Enough to poison a whole monastery of novices! You'd better wash your hands.'

The door slammed open behind them. Charlie flinched. Balthazar melted into the shadows.

'Hey, you,' shouted a turnspit. 'Eadgyth wants to know what you're up to in 'ere. She says she needs that nutmeg today, not tomorrow.'

Charlie was shaking. What if Sturgeon was the murderer? How could he calmly go about his tasks in the kitchen when the murderer might be standing right next to him?

He had to keep calm, keep his head. What had Eadgyth wanted? The spidery labels swam in front of his eyes. He grabbed a few jars from the nearest shelf and fled from the room, crashing headlong into Eadgyth, who was just coming in through the door.

'Have I got to come and get them ingredients myself?' she grumbled. 'Shove over – what have you got there? I never said I wanted no fennel seeds.'

She landed Charlie a sharp slap on his right ear, sending him spinning backwards into a barrel of almonds.

'Go and help them two pot boilers with the whisking. Take a turn for once. I don't know what's got into you today,' she snapped, slamming out of the room.

'What's got into her, more like,' hissed Balthazar, reappearing from behind a pot of pickled gherkins.

'There's something funny going on,' said Charlie in a shocked voice, holding his smarting ear. 'Why is she so angry with me? It's not like her.'

'You only say that because she's usually nice to you. You know she can be as sour as she is sweet.'

Charlie's head was reeling. Nothing made sense. Could Sturgeon be the poisoner? And if the culprit was Sturgeon, why would he want to steal recipes?

The rest of the morning flew by in a flurry of chopping and crushing, whisking and puréeing. Eadgyth was snapping at everyone and her mood wasn't improved by accidentally chopping her finger instead of a dried fig. The scullions breathed a sigh of relief when she went off howling with Erik to the infirmary.

Eadgyth and Erik were gone for some time, but when they came back she was more her usual self. Charlie tried hard to behave normally and concentrate on his work. Balthazar was nowhere to be seen.

The ox that had been roasting since early morning was giving off a delicious meaty aroma, and yeasty smells of barley bread wafted across from the bakehouse. The cake grew taller, tier upon sumptuous tier of sponge and exotic fruits soaked in wine. Eadgyth was absorbed in her craft, adding a touch of honey here, removing a spot of cream there.

Erik was modelling animals out of marzipan for the top layer – a stag with a cavity in the middle to be filled with red wine as a surprise for Lady Goslar. When she bit into it, the wine would come spurting out – like blood from a wound!

'What do we do after this?' Charlie panted to Erik from the top of a set of wooden steps. He was ladling the last bowl of cinnamon cream on to the final layer of the cake. 'I'm exhausted.'

'Too bad, Charlie! We've got another job. You and me's to go to the rocky beach to collect oysters. Sturgeon's orders. I'll just go and collect the ropes and pails from the boathouse. Gotta go now to catch the low tide.'

25
Oyster Pie

'What have you brought the ropes for?' panted Charlie, struggling with four large oyster pails.

'You'll see,' replied Erik, striding out.

Low tide had brought out the wading birds, oystercatchers and red shanks with legs the colour of sealing wax.

'Why do we need oysters, anyway?' moaned Charlie. 'Surely there's enough food already.'

Erik looked horrified. 'No oysters for her Ladyship's birthday? Lady Goslar always has venison-and-oyster pie for her birthday.'

'How do we get down to the beach? I don't see a path,' said Charlie.

'That's cos there isn't one,' grunted Erik. He grinned at Charlie. 'You scared of heights?'

'Course I'm not scared,' he gulped. 'What do we have to do then?'

'Well, we've got two ropes, one for you and one for me.

You tie this end of the rope around your waist and this end around one of these 'ere trees. It's only for safety, mind. You shouldn't fall – there are plenty of footholds on the way.'

The beach looked a long way down, and the rocks were jagged and sharp. This must be near the hermit's cave, thought Charlie. What an odd place for him to live.

A cormorant shot blackly across the waves as Charlie and Erik began to scramble down the scrubby cliff top to the edge, where the cliff face fell steeply away down to the beach. Charlie closed his eyes and turned his back to the sea. Best not look, he thought. Don't look up; don't look down. His heart was thumping. Erik seemed quite at ease, as agile as a monkey. He's probably done this hundreds of times before, thought Charlie apprehensively.

They'd been climbing downwards for some time in silence. Pieces of rock from above rained down on their heads and Charlie's mouth was full of grit mixed with blood where he had bitten his lip in concentration. He was just gaining confidence when all of a sudden Erik shouted.

'Help! Charlie! My foot's stuck!'

Charlie glanced across at Erik. His left leg was skewed out at an awkward angle and he was clinging to the cliff face, looking petrified.

'Quick! You've got to help me. I'm losing my grip. My other leg can't take the weight!'

'Oh, great!' yelled Charlie. 'I've got enough to do looking after myself!' His fingers were cut and bleeding, numb with cold. 'Hold on,' he called. 'I'll try and shuffle across. Just hang on tight – I'm coming.'

Erik was whimpering now, clinging on to the cliff face. Steadying himself with his left hand, Charlie reached out shakily to grasp Erik's foot. Suddenly the trapped foot shot out, catching Charlie a hefty blow on the shoulder. And the next moment he was falling, hurtling down the cliff face. There was an almighty tug on the rope around his waist followed by a sharp crack, then the noise of splintering wood, the sickening groan of branches and the snapping of twigs. It was as if hundreds of knives were piercing his body. He felt a searing agony in his head, and then nothing.

Hours passed before Charlie came round at last. It was dark. Every muscle in his body ached, and his head was throbbing. He struggled in and out of consciousness. In his waking moments he was in dreadful pain but, more than that, he was troubled by something nagging at the edge of his mind, something important. He didn't know how he'd ended up lying in the branches of a stunted tree, sprouting from the side of the cliff. The bush had broken his fall. His safety rope had snapped and the end, still tied around his waist, dangled forlornly down, twirling gently.

Little by little he began to remember fragments of what had happened: the climb down the cliff face, the piercing cold, and then Erik's foot as it shot out towards him. And suddenly it came to him, the disturbing thing that he had been struggling to remember. It was the expression on Erik's face in that split second before he had lost his grip. It was a look of pure hatred mingled with satisfaction. And at last Charlie realized the truth. This was no accident! But why should Erik hate him enough to try to kill him? Only one thing was clear. Charlie was trapped on the cliff side, helpless to save himself or even raise the alarm.

Up in her turret room, Marian was feeling peeved. She'd been furious with Charlie all afternoon and now evening had come she had made up her mind. Why should she go out alone on a freezing winter's night to keep a watch on the library? All Charlie had to do was look up the toadstools in the book she'd given him and have a go at translating the riddle. Hardly a fair division of labour.

'How dare he order me about?' she grumbled to herself. 'He's just a scullion in my father's kitchens. If he's too busy cooking, then I'm too busy at the banquet. Mother will be disappointed if I don't go to her birthday feast. Whatever happens in the library this evening can happen without me,' she muttered as she drooped gloomily down the uneven stairs.

Alone in his study Father Bernard sat huddled in his cloak before the blazing hearth, his shadow huge on the wall in the candlelight. He wriggled his toes painfully in his fur-lined slippers. In his hand he held his translation of the runic riddle.

I am a tutor not in human form,
Though wrought by man and made of skin was not of woman born.

'That must mean that the thing the riddle refers to is

something that teaches, but is not a person. What is not a person, but also made of skin?'

Though leaves I have I am yet not a tree,
Though pages serve yet no man kneels to me.

'Leaves and pages but not leaves of a tree, and not pages that serve a king. Leaves and pages and skin – it's a book! Books give us information and have leaves and pages and parchment is made of goatskin.' He read on.

'"Delve deep within my leafy heart" – that must mean, read me – "and I'll reveal to thee, the secrets traced upon my skin – a tasty alchemy". The secrets traced upon my skin – that must mean the writing, and that the writing is something to do with alchemy. Now, alchemy is the science of turning base metals into gold, or trying to, but a tasty alchemy? What could that mean?'

He frowned and scratched his head. Where on earth had Marian found this strange riddle? Was it just a bit of fun, or did it have a more serious meaning? He had an uneasy feeling about it. He got up stiffly and crossed to the window. How dark it was, and yet there was the moon emerging from the clouds, almost full but not quite, as if the tiniest slice had been pared away.

'Good Lord!' he exclaimed. He'd agreed with Abbot Gregory to keep a guard on the library tonight because of last night's full moon! He'd become so absorbed in solving the riddle that he had forgotten the time. The great abbey bell sounded. He glanced at his water clock, patiently dripping away the minutes.

Charlie lay frozen, delirious on the cliff side. At first he had tried to cry out for help, but a crushing pain in his ribs ripped through him every time he drew even the shallowest breath. His head was throbbing horribly. Desperately thirsty, he opened his mouth to catch the fine drizzle that was falling in a mist on to his face. He slipped back into blissful unconsciousness, that glorious place where there was no pain.

The library was a long gallery on the ground floor of the monastery. There was only one approach to it from the outside, since its east wall overlooked the sea. Father Bernard decided to conceal himself in the orchard, from where he would have a good view of the library entrance. He gained the cover of the apple trees and crouched painfully down behind a mature trunk. He was out of breath and oddly excited.

It was surprisingly noisy in the orchard, rain dripping off the bare branches of the fruit trees and plopping on to the piles of rotting leaves below. He shifted his position. It wasn't easy for an elderly monk to squat in the damp like a fugitive. He heard a sudden sharp intake of breath nearby, somewhere between a gasp and a muffled scream.

'Father Bernard! What on earth are you doing here?'

Father Bernard scrambled stiffly to his feet, feeling rather foolish.

'Ahem … I could quite properly ask the same question of you, Lady Marian.'

'Oh, I'd had enough of the feast, that's all,' she explained hurriedly. 'Mother was ridiculous, stuffing buns and birthday cake, and the mummers were boring. I've seen it all before.'

'That still doesn't explain why you're creeping around in a damp garden in the dark. How many times do I have to warn you, young lady? There's a murderer –'

A cry stopped him in mid-sentence.

'Did you hear that?' hissed Father Bernard. They stared at each other in alarm.

'I heard something,' whispered Marian, 'but it sounded like an animal. Did it come from the library? Wait …' she grasped his cloak. 'There it is again. It's someone crying for help! Where's it coming from?'

Father Bernard hurried towards an arched opening in the garden wall. The noise of the sea was deafening but there was the cry again, unmistakably human and much clearer now, carried towards them on the wind.

'It's coming from down on the beach,' cried Marian. 'Someone's in trouble. Quick. I know a path, but it's very slippery. I hope it's not too steep for you, Father.' But Father Bernard had already hitched up his cloak and begun the treacherous descent.

At last Marian and Father Bernard reached the beach. The cries for help were louder now, still intermittent but much closer. Marian was running as fast as the slippery rocks would allow, across the sand towards the cry. Father Bernard lumbered along behind her, determined to keep up. They had reached the base of the cliff, which rose straight up from the shore.

'It's coming from up there – right above our heads. Look,

Father Bernard! Do you see that glow? That broken old tree – it's almost as if it were on fire!'

'Help me, somebody, help!'

'It's Charlie! Quick, Father Bernard,' Marian screamed. 'It's Charlie's voice coming from that twisted old tree. Charlie, Charlie! Hold on – we're here. It's me, Marian! Charlie, speak to me. Are you hurt? We're down here on the beach. We've come to help you.'

26
Father Simeon

'**M**ake haste with the stretcher, boys,' called Father Bernard urgently. His black habit, sodden with rain, clung to his legs as he strode through the cloisters directing the rescue party of young monks. 'Father Simeon is expecting us. I sent Lady Marian on ahead to warn him of the accident.'

'They're here at last, Father Simeon,' called Marian in relief, flinging open the infirmary door and springing out with a lantern to light their way. 'What took you so long?' she cried.

'This way, boys,' commanded Father Bernard brusquely, pushing past Marian. She flattened herself against the wall of the narrow corridor to let them squeeze by with the jolting stretcher. Charlie groaned in pain.

'I was as swift as I could be, Marian,' snapped Father Bernard, mopping his brow. 'I had to rouse the rescue party from their beds and it was no easy task to bring him down from the cliff side.'

'Charlie. It's me, Marian!' she cried, darting to his side. 'Everything's going to be all right.'

'Bring the child this way,' called Father Simeon, scuttling out of the pharmacy like a black beetle. 'Brother Dominic – you will stay behind to assist me with the invalid. The rest of you may leave.'

'He's going to be all right isn't he, Father Simeon?' begged Marian.

'That decision is in the hands of the Almighty, my dear,' replied Father Simeon gravely, gently pulling back the bloodstained fabric of Charlie's tunic. A jagged flesh wound snaked across his stomach. Charlie screamed. 'I fear this wound has exposed the bone and he has lost a prodigious amount of blood.'

'He's not going to die, is he?' wailed Marian.

'If it is God's will that he should die, then so be it,' barked Father Simeon, 'but just now I could get along better if you were not standing on my toe!'

Charlie lay shivering, whimpering with pain and fear. A small fire burned in the grate of the simple whitewashed room. His face and lips were badly lacerated by the branches of the bush that had saved his life. One eye was swollen and closed and a dribble of blood mixed with saliva ran from the corner of his mouth. Father Simeon's arthritic old hands worked deftly.

'What's that you're mixing, Father Simeon?' sniffed Marian, trying not to cry.

'Horehound and myrtle mixed with a little lavender oil to bind his wounds,' replied Father Simeon tetchily, elbowing her to one side. 'I'm sorry, my dear, but you really are in the way. Pass me that jar of spiders' webs, Brother Dominic. I will lay them on top of the wound to aid the healing process.'

'I'm sorry,' said Marian. 'I just want to do something to help.'

'The best way you can help is by not placing yourself between me and the oil lamp. My eyes are dim at the best of times. Go with Brother Dominic and beat up some egg whites and milk. When I've finished dressing his wounds you can try and get him to drink something.'

Father Bernard craned his head around the door. 'How is the child, Simeon?'

'Very weak indeed, Bernard. His breathing is poor and his pulse is slow.'

He stumbled over Marian's feet again.

'Oh, for heaven's sake, take Lady Marian away!' he exploded. 'Go away, child. I will call you when I have finished.'

'Come, Marian,' said Father Bernard gently. 'I need to speak with you anyway,' he continued, lowering his voice. 'Am I right in assuming that this young scullion is the boy you were telling me about the other day?'

'Yes, Father,' gulped Marian, wiping a tear away with the back of her hand, and looking distractedly back at Charlie.

'But I thought you said he had disappeared!' whispered Father Bernard. 'Come up to my study,' he said more loudly. 'There should be a good fire burning, and I for one would like to dry my clothes. Father Simeon will bring us word if there is any change in the boy.'

Huddled in her cloak in Father Bernard's study, Marian had almost finished her tale of Charlie's return from Viking times with news of the holy hand. Charlie had urged her to trust no one, but she couldn't go on any longer worrying about all this alone.

'I didn't believe him at first, but after he vanished before my eyes in the church I had to trust him. When we met again on the cliff side, he was covered in cuts and bruises and … and he had a golden cross with him. He said it belonged to Saint Oswald, so naturally I told him about the holy hand at his shrine in the church. After that we decided we had to find a way to take a look at the relic – see if the ring really did contain a riddle.'

'Ahem,' coughed Father Bernard, looking grave. 'It seems you did rather more than look at it Marian. The hand of Saint Oswald is our blessed abbey's most precious treasure! Pilgrims crawl for miles on bleeding knees just to catch a glimpse of it. I'm sorry, my dear, but to imagine you children trespassing into the church and tampering with it – it makes me shudder.'

'But it did contain a riddle – just as Saint Oswald had told Charlie. So he was meant to find it wasn't he?' said Marian defensively. 'And the riddle contains the clue to the missing treasure!'

'I wish you had told me where that parchment came from in the first place, my dear,' said Father Bernard. 'If I had realized the importance of it, I would have consulted Abbot Gregory right away. And as if this were not enough, you say you have found some of the stolen recipes! Where did you find them, Marian, and where are they now? This might provide a clue to who has been stealing them.'

'I don't know – that's the problem,' she groaned. 'Charlie was looking after them. I think they must be hidden in the kitchens.'

'In the kitchens!' he exclaimed in disbelief. 'Oh, my dear girl! Surely you should have told somebody about them immediately. You really had no right to keep this vital information to yourselves, you know. A novice has been murdered, and the killer could strike again!'

Marian was looking shamefaced. Sitting in Father Bernard's study, with the firelight playing on his serious kindly face, she began to feel guilty about suspecting him of any wrongdoing.

'We thought we could try and find out who was drugging the novices and what killed poor Brother Harold. Charlie thinks the novices were given a potion made from the death cap toadstool. We'd seen a mysterious figure digging for them on the night I was caught by the mandrake root. But that's not what killed Brother Harold … Charlie thinks that he was killed by mouldy rye –'

'Toadstools, mandrake, whatever next!' exploded Father Bernard, passing an exasperated hand over his smooth tonsure. 'Really, Marian, this is too much to take in all at once. To say I am disturbed by these tidings is an understatement. The appearance of Saint Oswald in times of great peril is well known in the abbey. Could there be a link between these doleful happenings in the monastery and the riddle in his ring? I am now more fearful than ever about the evil that is abroad: drugging, poisoning, murder, and now this fearful accident, if accident it be!'

27
Almond Cakes

ews of Charlie's accident reached the kitchen
by midday. Everyone had risen late after Lady
Goslar's party. The remains of her birthday cake
lay in a desolate heap on the table, a snoring turnspit face
down in one of its creamy layers.

'I was looking for Charlie all afternoon,' moaned
Barnacle mournfully. 'I wanted to show 'im me nose.'

'Oh, bother your nose, Barnacle!' exclaimed Eadgyth.
'Can't you never think of nobody but yourself? The poor
boy's dying in the infirmary, and all you can think about
is your warts.'

'He might get better,' said Barnacle indignantly.

'Oooh, I don't think so! Them injuries is fatal – Erik said
so.'

Erik, gloomily sweeping out the hearths, kept his eyes
lowered.

'Eadgyth!' Sturgeon was on the warpath again. 'Where's
that barrel of butter?' he yelled, striding into the group.

'And what's all this blubbing about? Got no work to do?'
He grabbed Barnacle by the ear and twisted it cruelly.
'Now, where 'ave you been? I want a new lock put on
my spice-cupboard door – immediately! Somebody ...'
he growled, looking menacingly around him, 'has been
making free with my herbs and spices what's got no right
to them.'

Charlie lay in bed in the infirmary, the wound in his side
throbbing angrily. It smelt awful. His mother would have
used the carpenter's herb, the self-heal plant, but maybe it
didn't grow in these parts. Perhaps they didn't even know
about it. What if a fever took hold of him and he had to rely
on these monks and their primitive medicine? What if he
died far away from home and in another time?

Charlie's mind was in turmoil. He was desperate to speak
to Balthazar. He struggled in vain to remember when he
last saw the cat but his thoughts were jumbled. Who could
he trust to tell about Sturgeon and the toadstools? And
surely he should tell somebody about Erik too!

'There's something odd about all this,' he whispered
fretfully to himself. 'Why is Erik in league with Sturgeon?
It just doesn't make sense!'

'Psst! Charlie!'

Balthazar was crouching on the window ledge, peeping
anxiously around the latticework shutter. A flurry of
snowflakes fluttered down on to the rush floor as he pushed
it inwards. An icy blast engulfed the bed.

'Balthazar! Where were you when I needed you?'
Charlie almost wept with relief. 'I've been in real danger.

Something terrible has happened – Erik tried to kill me! I thought I was going to die!'

'I know, Charlie,' said Balthazar, passing a distracted paw over his bedraggled whiskers. 'I came as soon as I could but I've only just heard. I've been trapped in the boathouse all night – sick with worry. I escaped only a few minutes ago. I raced to the kitchens to find you and then I heard the news. Everyone's talking about the accident, even that wretch Erik. He's there, calm as anything, sweeping out the hearths as if butter wouldn't melt in his mouth!'

'So how do you know about Erik?' said Charlie, bewildered. 'My head's spinning.'

'Because I saw him fray the ropes! I followed him when he went to fetch them from the boathouse. I had a sixth sense something was afoot – something odd about that last-minute change of plan to go to the beach to collect oysters. When he started interfering with the ropes I knew something awful was going to happen – and I was helpless to stop it!'

'I nearly fell to my death!' exploded Charlie.

'But I couldn't warn you,' hissed Balthazar defensively. 'I told you – I was trapped! I was having a good snoop round looking for clues and I heard the door bang shut behind me. Erik turned the key and I was stuck. I only managed to escape just now because somebody came to collect a pair of oars. I came as soon as I could. Sturgeon's behind all this. He must be. He sent you off with Erik to collect oysters.'

'But why, Balthazar? Why should Sturgeon want to kill me?'

'There's only one explanation, Charlie. He thought you'd discovered the truth! Don't forget, Erik saw you return on the night of the mandrake root. It must have been Sturgeon out gathering toadstools and then Erik told him you'd seen him. Maybe Erik told him about that toadstool you accidentally left in the basket of goose eggs. Erik was there when Eadgyth found it. He must have thought you were on Sturgeon's trail and told him so!'

'But he couldn't have known I'd found the string of toadstools in his spice store. We were in there alone, Balthazar!'

'Visitors, Charlie,' beamed Father Simeon, tiptoeing into his room with a small tray of almond cakes sent over from the castle kitchens. He placed them by his bedside next to a steaming bowl of honey broth.

Balthazar cringed back behind the shutter.

'I'm hoping you might feel up to taking a little nourishment, my dear,' he said, heaving Charlie up against a bolster. 'And here are Lady Marian and Father Bernard come to talk to you. Not so boisterous with the patient, my dear,' scolded Father Simeon. 'Be careful, Marian! You will knock his broth over. Come, Charlie,' he said, offering him an almond cake. 'You must have something to eat and drink. You can talk at the same time.'

Charlie was looking confused.

'This is Father Bernard, Charlie,' said Father Simeon reassuringly. 'He led the rescue party last night.'

'Lady Marian has told me all about your, er ... how shall we put it ... your wanderings,' said Father Bernard uneasily. 'I would like to ask a few questions if I may.'

'I've … I've told him about the riddle and the ring,' Marian blurted out guiltily. 'I know we said we wouldn't, but I had to! And Charlie … when we found you on the cliff side, there was an orange light. Father Bernard says I was imagining it, but I know I saw a halo of light.'

'I wasn't alone, Marian,' he smiled. 'Saint Oswald was with me.'

'Saint Oswald!' breathed Marian. She looked triumphantly at the astonished Father Bernard.

'You had a vision of Saint Oswald, my child?' asked Father Bernard, his eyes widening. 'And … and did he speak to you? I … I am lost for words. Lady Marian told me that she had seen a light around the bush but … you had better explain, my child.' He took a deep breath. 'Tell me – what did Saint Oswald have to say to you?'

'He told me to have courage … that help was coming and that I had to hold on … to life I suppose, because I had some important work to do.'

'What sort of work, my child?' prompted Father Bernard.

'He said I could help Abbot Gregory restore some long-lost relics to the abbey,' said Charlie uncertainly, 'stop them falling into the wrong hands. I don't suppose for a moment you believe me.'

'Oh, I am afraid I do, my child,' he said, fiddling nervously with the sleeve of his habit. 'This is not the first time visions of Saint Oswald have been seen at times of crisis.'

Charlie found talking exhausting, but he managed to outline his suspicions to the kindly old librarian, the discovery of the string of poisonous toadstools in Sturgeon's spice room, and his belief that Erik had tried to kill him.

'I don't understand why he had it in for me,' gasped Charlie painfully. 'I assume Sturgeon must have thought that I knew what he was up to. It was he who sent me to gather oysters with Erik. They must be in it together, although that bit doesn't make much sense to me. But it was definitely no accident. I didn't slip at all – I was pushed!'

Father Bernard had risen to his feet and was preparing to leave at once.

'This is grave news indeed, my child. Marian has already told me that you believe the novices were poisoned – the death cap toadstool, am I right? And a string of them in Sturgeon's spice store certainly points the finger of suspicion in his direction. And now you say he sent you to your death! I am still struggling with the meaning of the riddle found in Saint Oswald's ring. I am sure it is a vital clue to these dreadful events, but I am afraid the riddle will have to wait its turn. I must make haste to inform Abbot Gregory of your suspicions immediately. Who knows, the villain Sturgeon may even now be planning another victim's fate!'

'Perhaps Charlie could help out with the riddle while you're seeing the abbot,' suggested Marian. 'He's really clever, Father Bernard,' she added loyally. 'He can read Latin and Greek.'

Father Bernard cleared his throat uncomfortably. Could this kitchen boy really know how to read?

'Well,' he said distractedly, his hand already on the latch, 'it can do no harm for you to have a look, I suppose. I have a rough translation of the riddle here but I am blessed if I can decipher the last part of it. Now, Simeon, not a word to anyone about the culprit, Sturgeon – not until I have consulted Abbot Gregory. He will advise me what to do for the best.'

As the door closed behind him, Marian settled herself more comfortably on the bed. Charlie sank back against the bolster

'Oh no you don't, Lady Marian,' said Father Simeon sternly. 'You must go too. Charlie is tired.'

Charlie pressed his hand against his clammy forehead. He was feeling unwell again and yet he was curious to see Father Bernard's translation.

'Oh, just a few more minutes, Father Simeon,' pleaded Marian. 'Let's see if Charlie can understand the riddle.'

The infirmarian heaved an indulgent sigh. 'Two minutes only then, but I will remain here. Now, Charlie, eat this last almond cake before you start,' he fussed. 'We need to build up your strength.'

Charlie began to read silently, the corners of his lips turning up in a little smile of understanding.

'I ... I ... think I might understand it,' he ventured modestly. 'I'm sure the first part of the riddle refers to a book, but what's meant by "a tasty alchemy"?'

'Don't look at me,' said Marian. 'I'm no scholar!'

'Do you suppose it could refer to something edible – a kind of magic where things are mixed up together and become something else, something you can taste or eat?'

'Like cooking?' offered Father Simeon tentatively.

'Ye-es, I suppose so – like a recipe, where the ingredients

are combined together until they become something more than the sum of their parts.'

'"I came from the dark earth and there I shall remain",' read Father Simeon, eagerly peering over Charlie's shoulder. 'It can't be so difficult. I presume the writer wanted somebody to work it out!'

'If the riddle is something to do with lost treasure, then it must be the treasure itself that came from the dark earth originally, and now lies hidden in it again.'

'You mean things like gold and silver and valuable gems?' said Marian excitedly. 'Just imagine if we could find it!'

Charlie nodded. 'Yes, and things made out of them. Now – let's see. "My whereabouts a letter doth conceal, which when eaten doth provide a tasty meal."'

'References to food again. How deliciously intriguing,' said Father Simeon, casting an anxious look at Charlie. The boy was looking rather grey. 'But does that mean we need to go off hunting for a letter now?'

'Oh, that sort of letter?' said Charlie, looking up. 'I hadn't thought of it in that way. You may be right, Father, but I … I don't think so. I think it refers to pi,' he continued. 'The sixteenth letter of the Greek alphabet! A letter which when eaten provides a tasty meal!'

'But that doesn't make sense, does it?' snorted Marian, disappointed. 'How can the whereabouts of the monastery treasure be hidden in a pie?'

'Not in a pie itself,' replied Charlie, 'that would be rather messy! But perhaps in a recipe for one.' He dropped the parchment suddenly. 'That's it, Marian! The motive!' he cried excitedly. 'The missing link! We were right. The secret of the ring has everything to do with the poisoning of the novices! We've assumed that whoever has been stealing recipes wanted them for their own sake. But the recipes are nothing in themselves, except that they contain a clue ... to the location of the treasure! And talking of food I feel ...' Charlie suddenly clutched at his stomach.

'What is it, child?' said Father Simeon, alarmed. 'Is the pain so great? Marian, dear, I fear I must ask you to leave.'

Charlie was looking much worse. Beads of perspiration stood out on his pale forehead. He groaned aloud as Marian slipped out of the door.

It started with severe stomach cramps, and then the itching began.

28
Betrayal

U p in his draughty study Abbot Gregory listened in silence to Father Bernard's strange news. They had drawn up their chairs to the hearth.

'My dear Bernard, have you taken leave of your senses?' spluttered Abbot Gregory incredulously. 'Sturgeon from the kitchens? Are you really expecting me to believe that an unknown scullion has exposed the murderer of our unfortunate novice?'

'Well ... I –'

'And that this same scullion has travelled back into the past and met the long-dead Saint Oswald? And do you believe Lady Marian's bizarre stories? You know as well as I do that she is a strange and lonely child, and these claims are far-fetched to say the very least!'

'I quite agree, my dear Gregory, but it is not only Lady Marian's tale. I have met this young boy myself and he is a most persuasive child. His description of the sack of the Saxon settlement all those years ago is most convincing.

How could a boy like that have such a detailed knowledge of those happenings?'

'And what is the story about the parchment and the ring? You had better explain everything to me from the beginning, Bernard.'

There was a soft knocking on the oak door. 'Enter,' cried the abbot.

'Excuse me, Abbot Gregory,' stammered a nervous young novice, 'but there's a boy called Erik from the kitchens here. He says he needs to see you. Says it's urgent.'

'Indeed?' said the abbot. 'You'd better show him in.'

The novice stepped aside and Erik skulked in, his thin foxy face and greasy hair a marked contrast to the two well-groomed monks.

'Now, what can we do for you, young man? I do hope this is no silly prank,' warned Abbot Gregory.

Father Bernard put another log on the fire. So this was Erik, the miserable little scullion Charlie had told him about. He would allow the abbot to hear the villain out, before letting on that he knew all about his treachery.

Erik had come to betray Sturgeon, and the abbot had been listening patiently for some time to his tales.

'This is a very serious allegation against the master chef, young man,' interrupted Abbot Gregory. 'You say that Sturgeon gave you the frayed ropes on purpose so that Charlie Ferret would fall to his death?'

'He knew Charlie suspected him and he wanted him out of the way. Sturgeon's been poisoning them novices what've been guarding the Book and stealing the pages for months now, to get ideas for his own cooking. He'd found Charlie with some of the stolen recipes. We were best friends, me and Charlie. I did what I could to save him, but I might have fallen meself.'

'But didn't Sturgeon suspect you too, being such friends?' asked the abbot. 'Why didn't he try to kill you both at the same time?'

'Oh, I think he thought I'd be too scared of him to tell! But that Charlie Ferret, he don't seem to care what people think of him and he's friends with Lady Marian from the castle.'

'But what proof do you have, young man?' asked the abbot.

'If you don't believe me, you look at his strings of mushrooms in his spice store. Won't you get a surprise?'

Father Bernard had risen to his feet – his hands were trembling. 'You were with Charlie, were you not, when he met with his accident?'

'Oh, I was there all right! I saw my dearest friend falling to his death. "Charlie!" I screamed, but it was too late.'

'And so you immediately rushed to summon help?' Father Bernard's voice was steely cold, his eyes hostile.

'Er … not exactly, you see I …'

An owl screeched, hunting for its prey. Father Bernard was edging closer to Erik.

'Abbot,' said Father Bernard icily, 'we must see Lord Goslar at once. We need his authority to search the kitchens, and you, boy, not a word to anyone about what you have just told us, do you hear? If your information results in the arrest of the culprit, you will be rewarded.'

Father Bernard had almost reached the wretch. Erik was

feeling relieved. The interview had gone better than he had dared hope, when suddenly Father Bernard lunged, grabbing him by the jerkin and twisting his right arm behind him. 'Gotcha, you treacherous little devil! We weren't born yesterday, you know. I know what you've been up to, you lying little toad!'

'Father Bernard!' exclaimed the abbot in shocked tones. 'Good heavens, man, what language! Remember your Holy Orders.'

Father Bernard's face was white; two small spots of scarlet on each cheekbone.

'This, Abbot Gregory, is the snivelling little creature that pushed our friend Charlie down the cliff side, and now he comes trying to pretend he isn't Sturgeon's minion, giving us "useful information", when all the while he's trying to save his own skin!' He twisted Erik's arm so that the boy cried out.

'Calm yourself, Bernard,' said the abbot. 'Put the boy down for a moment. You'll break his arm. How can we be sure the boy is not –'

A sharp knock on the door. 'Enter,' cried the abbot impatiently.

'Oh, Father Bernard, you're wanted in the infirmary,' gabbled a novice. 'It's the injured scullion. He's much worse!'

Father Bernard had only slightly relaxed his hold on Erik, but it was enough. Erik seized his chance. Wrenching himself from Father Bernard's grasp, he was out of the window and shinning down the ivy before the old priest had time to notice that all he was holding in his hand was an empty jerkin.

29
Essence of Roast Viper

Sturgeon was settling down contentedly to a quiet supper of roast curlews' eggs and minced sparrows. His bloodshot eyes glinted greedily as he sloshed strong wine into his earthenware tankard. He loosened his leather belt and sat down with a grunt, listening contentedly to the clattering of the scullions clearing up in the kitchen.

At first he didn't realize anything was wrong. He was used to arguments – probably another row between Barnacle and Erik. A happy belch escaped his lips. But wasn't that Weazel's voice shouting above the others? He heaved his chair back angrily.

'What's going on?' he roared. 'Can't a man 'ave 'is dinner in peace?'

Weazel skidded around the corner, his monkey arms flailing.

'Sturgeon, oh, Sturgeon, sir! They're a-coming for you. Six castle guards – coming to arrest you. They say you poisoned them novices!'

Sturgeon's ruddy face drained of all colour. A thread of gravy dribbled down his stubbly chin.

'Me?' he bellowed, bits of half-chewed sparrow flying. 'What do you mean? There must be some mistake! Clear off, you wizened monkey. If this is some kind of a joke I'll –'

Chain mail rattled as the guards marched through the kitchens to where Sturgeon was waiting in disbelief. Scullions and turnspits crowded in behind the guards, sweaty faces shining in the torchlight.

'Here he is, the vicious murderer!' cried one of the guards. 'Seize him!'

Eadgyth began to whimper, her hand to her mouth. Barnacle put a protective arm around her. Sturgeon's pale face twitched, but his hand was steady as he reached for the meat cleaver.

Sturgeon awoke in the dungeons next morning to the delicious aroma of the breakfast he'd meant for himself. Scrumptious smells of fried bacon mingled oddly with the stink of decay and rotten unwashed flesh. He tried to move, but his bonds held him firm, chained to the damp wall with water dripping down his neck. His temple was red and swollen, his right eye shiny and black. He hadn't come quietly. It had taken all six guards to overpower the master chef and his whirling blade.

''Ere … come and let me out, someone!' bellowed Sturgeon. 'You can't keep me 'ere like a common sheep-stealer.'

'Shut yer face!' The crippled gaoler swung into view on his crutches. 'What's it to be for yer breakfast, Sturgeon? A nice juicy partridge in a cherry sauce, ha ha ha!' He poked Sturgeon with his crutch. 'Think you should be treated different from the rest of 'em, do ya? Well, we're all the same down here and I'm in charge. We all stay here nice and quiet, we do, while we waits for us ordeals. What's it to be for you, eh? A nice gentle stretch on the rack until your bones crack and you confess?'

'But I haven't done nothing wrong!' blustered Sturgeon. 'I need to speak to Lady Goslar. I'm the chief cook, the great Sturgeon. What will Lady Goslar do without her almond puffs, and it's only me as knows how to make 'em!'

'Shurrup. You've been caught red-handed, you have,' taunted the gaoler. 'Poisoned toadstools in your larder, so them guards say.' He sniffed, a malicious grin spreading over his face. 'Now, is that bacon what I can smell?'

Charlie lay on his bed writhing in pain, vomiting and retching so that the wound in his side opened up and bled afresh. He tore constantly at a blotchy rash that covered his skin from head to foot. Charlie was either possessed by a devil or he had been poisoned, and Father Simeon was convinced it was poisoning. The symptoms were identical to those suffered by Brother Harold, before the poor child had died in agony.

Father Simeon pored over his lists of herbs in the pharmacy, desperately searching for inspiration, his black cauldron simmering above the hearth – bulls' blood and goose droppings, his latest cure for fits. But what could have caused such intense irritation? He couldn't understand it. The boy had been convalescing so well! He shuffled back into the sickroom, and sat down wearily on the bed.

'Don't call my mother a witch!' screamed Charlie.

Father Simeon shivered and crossed himself. He could sense the boy's strength ebbing away by the minute. If he couldn't think of something soon, Charlie would surely die too.

A mouse was nibbling at some crumbs of cake on the empty trencher in the hearth. Father Simeon could do with some ground mouse bones. He made a lunge for it, but his stiff old body was too slow. He picked up the trencher. That was another curious thing. Charlie had felt hungry enough to eat a whole batch of cakes from the kitchens, and then he had suddenly collapsed.

Father Simeon dropped the trencher in excitement. Of course! The cakes! Why had he taken so long to realize it? Surely he had seen enough cases of rye poisoning in his time. There'd been an epidemic of it some years ago. The symptoms were coming back to him now, the intense itching, mad ravings. It had to be the cakes – they must have contained rye flour, contaminated with a deadly fungus. Now, what remedy had they used for it then?

He scuttled back to the pharmacy, rummaging anxiously in the back of his catalogue, tearing the fragile parchment in his haste. There, in a steadier, younger hand was the formula he'd been searching for.

Shakily he climbed the ladder to the topmost shelf, a candle clutched in his hand. Ah, yes, thank God, here was the fellow he was after; a tiny ancient yellow pot, its faded label almost illegible in the guttering candlelight.

'"Powdered essence of Roast Viper",' he read.

30
The Cellar of the Ancient Volumes

Father Bernard and Abbot Gregory were in the library, the shutters flung back, pale afternoon light streaming in through the round-headed windows.

'The news from the infirmary is grave indeed, Bernard,' said the abbot grimly. 'Father Simeon tells me he thinks he has discovered the cause of the boy's present affliction, but he regrets that it may by now be too late.'

'And yet it is this poor injured scullion that we have to thank for the solution to the riddle in the ring,' said Father Bernard sorrowfully. 'Father Simeon tells me he solved the riddle in moments last evening, just after I had left him to bring you news of the villain Sturgeon, and only minutes before he collapsed!'

'Thank heavens the evil scoundrel is safely imprisoned in the dungeons,' replied the abbot, 'and at least the poor child could not be in more capable hands than Simeon's. Of that I have no doubt. But tell me more about this riddle, Bernard. I have read your translation with care, but what does it mean?'

'Well, abbot, it seems that the riddle links a recipe for some kind of pie to the lost monastery treasure. It would appear that the clue to its whereabouts is to be found within a recipe book. It would explain everything – the poisonings and the theft of the pages from our sacred volume.'

The abbot looked unconvinced. 'It is an intriguing idea, Bernard,' he said doubtfully, 'but it by no means explains everything. There is one major problem you have overlooked. If the boy is correct that the reference to a book containing "tasty alchemy" is to a recipe book, we need to find a recipe book even older than our own Great Book – one that was around in Saint Oswald's time. Our treasured Book is only about two hundred years old. The raids of the Norsemen in Oswald's lifetime were over three hundred years ago.'

'Aah! I see your point, Abbot,' said Father Bernard, looking a little downcast. 'I had not thought of that. You mean the recipes in our Book would not have existed at the time of Saint Oswald?'

'Indeed,' said the abbot. 'But I have an idea that would explain everything. You would agree, would you not, that everyone knows the story of Saint Oswald and the hidden treasure?'

'Of course, Abbot, it is a well-known tale,' confirmed Father Bernard. 'There are as many different legends about the treasure as there are stars in the heavens.'

'Quite so, Bernard – so this is my theory. Sturgeon is not an educated man. I believe he must have known of the legend of the treasure and its connection with a recipe book, and mistakenly believed that the clue to finding it lay concealed in our Great Recipe Book! He knew that Saint Oswald lived a long time ago. In that conviction, he decided to steal the oldest recipes from our sacred book first – the ones from the front – in the hope that he would eventually strike lucky and the location of the treasure would be revealed!'

'And all along, the villain was searching in the wrong book!' exclaimed Father Bernard in delight. 'And heaven be praised, he was!'

Abbot Gregory smiled. 'So now, my dear Bernard, to practicalities!' He scanned the dusty shelves. 'Are these the oldest volumes we have in the library, Bernard? Is it possible that we might have any recipe books which were written before our own Great Book?'

'It is quite possible, Abbot. The oldest volumes were taken inland for safety when the Norsemen came in Saint Oswald's time, but for many years now they have been stored in the cellar of the ancient volumes, beneath our own chapter house.'

'Excellent! Heavens, there goes the abbey bell,' exclaimed the abbot. 'It is time for prayers, but you may be excused the service, Bernard. I believe a visit to the cellar of the ancient volumes is in order, and the quicker it is accomplished, the better.'

As the two Fathers turned to leave they were taken aback to see a pale young monk emerge from behind a pillar.

'Oh, Brother Gilbert! You startled me,' cried the abbot. 'Where did you appear from? Watch where you're going! I nearly fell over you.'

* * * * *

Father Bernard was deep in thought as he strode through the shadowy cloister towards the circular building of the chapter house. It was late afternoon and the even plainsong of the monks at vespers echoed around the frosty pillars. He gave a start of surprise as Marian emerged from the gloom, her fur-lined hood almost covering her face.

'Marian, my dear,' gasped Father Bernard. 'Good heavens, you startled me. What are you up to, young miss? You look as if you've been crying.'

'I've just come from the infirmary,' sniffed Marian. 'Father Simeon won't let me stay and help with Charlie. He says I'm in the way. He's trying something new – roasted-viper paste or something.' She gave a watery little smile. 'It smells disgusting. Why aren't you at chapel, Father?'

'Well, as a matter of fact, I am engaged in a little investigation for Abbot Gregory concerning your riddle. Why don't you come along too?' he said kindly. 'It will occupy your mind for a while; stop you fretting over something you can do nothing about, my dear.'

The main door to the chapter house was locked, but a hidden staircase around the back led down to the cellar of the ancient volumes.

'Careful on the frosty steps, Marian,' warned Father Bernard, bending almost double to stoop under the lintel.

The smell was overpowering! Marian gagged audibly and put her hand over her mouth, squeezing her nostrils together.

'I'm sorry, Marian – I should have warned you,' said Father Bernard in a stifled voice. 'This is where the monks make our parchment. It's hard on the fingers and the nose!'

Marian took a deep breath of frosty air before ducking under the door frame after Father Bernard. Goatskins and sheepskins hung drying, softened first in urine. Some were stretched on racks where grey-robed novices patiently scraped the hairs off the skins.

The keeper of the ancient volumes was a pinched-faced little monk with a sallow pockmarked face, his skin the same colour as the parchment he so lovingly restored. He eyed Father Bernard suspiciously, sniffing and shaking his head nervously as he scuttled ahead of him, darting between the shelves and reappearing again some way ahead.

'Ahem ... a recipe book, did you say?' he said irritably.

The keeper reminded Father Bernard of a little mouse. He could hear him muttering to himself between the shelves – 'Mathematics, Medicine and Moths – no, not here. This is a bother you know. The novices and I are very busy cataloguing manuscripts.'

'I'm sorry if it's a nuisance, but if you would allow me to peruse the shelves by myself ...'

'Out of the question! And anyway, you're not by yourself,' he snapped waspishly, seeming to notice Marian for the first time. 'It is most, ahem, irregular to have a ... a,' he squinted at Marian, 'how shall I put it ... a girl in here.'

Marian made a move to go, eager to escape the stench, but Father Bernard put out a restraining hand.

'We need to examine the most ancient volumes in your possession, Brother – the ones that were rescued from the burning abbey in Saint Oswald's time.'

'Oh, well, that's it then!' he exclaimed, pushing past

Marian rudely. 'Can't help!'

'What do you mean, you can't help?'

'They're being mended, that's why,' he retorted, his eyes defiant. 'Falling apart. Some of the pages have just crumbled away. The novices are in charge of the repairs, but they're too busy to help you.'

'Who is too busy to help?' came a gentle voice from behind a wobbly tower of books. Its owner emerged, as plump and rosy-faced as the keeper of the volumes was thin and sallow.

'Oh, I didn't see you there,' said the keeper in a piqued voice. 'I was just telling Father Bernard that the oldest books couldn't be seen at the moment.'

'Why ever not, Brother?' said the novice. 'I would be happy to show Father Bernard the books I am mending. You are right, though. They are in dire need of repair and some of the pages are so badly stained with mildew as to be almost unreadable.' He selected a book from the stack. 'Here's the volume I am working on at the moment, for example. It is a work of Aristotle.'

Father Bernard fingered the fragile parchment. It smelled musty and very faintly of mushrooms, the writing faded and dull. The sheets had been gently lifted from their bindings and he gingerly picked one up, trying to decipher the script.

'This isn't quite what we had in mind, my child. Is there anything –'

'Father Bernard,' gasped Marian, 'look over here!'

She was blowing the dust from the damaged outer covers of a large book. 'I think it says something about pies, Father.'

'Of Pies, Pottages and Puddings,' exclaimed Father Bernard, his cry of triumph turning almost immediately to a moan of despair.

'Oh, that's just the outer binding, Father Bernard,' said the pleasant young monk. 'That was one of the volumes that had suffered most badly from mildew.'

'Can you remember what sort of recipes there were in this volume, my son?' asked Father Bernard, trying to hide his disappointment.

'Oh, yes, Father,' smiled the novice eagerly. 'I always read every book I work on. It makes the job so much more interesting and it helps me to forget the smell! Let's see now – there was one for roast fennel pottage, carp in coriander pastry, songbird pie …'

Father Bernard caught his breath.

'A pie, my child? A songbird pie?'

'Father Bernard,' cried Marian. 'Doesn't the riddle refer to birdsong?'

'Such a gruesome recipe,' said the novice, warming to his subject. 'The poor birds are put in the pie alive and then the pastry is cooked, but only enough to brown the top but not so much as to harm the birds. When it's cut open – the birds fly out and snuff out all the candles …'

'And where is this recipe, my child?' interrupted Father Bernard breathlessly. 'Can you show it to me?'

'Oh, I'm sorry, Father. The pages were so utterly beyond repair, I threw the damaged parchment away!'

31
Brother Gilbert

Father Simeon's small consulting room was full of black-robed figures huddled on benches, coughing and blowing their noses. The infirmarian chuckled to himself. Apart from the routine winter bloodlettings, there would be a stream of monks with mild head colds looking for a few days' rest in the infirmary. Hedge-mustard-and-horseradish cordial generally did the trick. They didn't come back in a hurry after a dose of that!

'No, no! Your throat is not in the least inflamed, but that back tooth needs pulling,' said Father Simeon briskly.

'Aaargh! Ow, ouch!'

'There you are,' grinned Father Simeon, holding up the offending tooth in a pair of pincers. 'Go and wash your mouth out with ale and stick this clove in the gap. Off you go – you'll be as frisky as a friar tomorrow!'

The consulting room emptied rapidly, furtive black figures slinking swiftly away without waiting for their turn. After a very short time there was only one patient left.

'Now, what can I do for you, Brother Gilbert?' he demanded.

Brother Gilbert stepped up, his shifty glance sliding around the room and back to Father Simeon. His breath was foul; Father Simeon could smell it from several feet away. There was something oddly repellent about this young man.

'It's the earache, Father,' he said clutching his face. 'I can hardly bear to move my head.' He made Father Simeon's flesh creep.

'I'd better have a peek,' said Father Simeon. 'Now, where did I put my pincers?'

'Pincers?' Brother Gilbert jumped back in alarm. Father Simeon grinned.

'Oh, not for you, don't upset yourself. Hmm now, let me see.'

He squinted into a rather grubby ear, infested with blackheads. Apart from a bit of grimy wax, the ear looked perfectly healthy.

'Have you been busy?' enquired the ginger monk. 'Er ... I heard there was somebody taken very sick.'

'We always minister to the sick here, Brother. Why do you ask?' said Father Simeon warily, resisting an urge to give his ear an extra-hard tweak. There was something about Brother Gilbert that he didn't like – too obsequious, that was it, but insolent at the same time: a curious mixture.

'I'm in dreadful pain, Father. I thought maybe you could keep me here under observation. Now, my old aunt had a boil in her ear that was that far down you couldn't see it, but –'

'Nonsense! There is nothing wrong with this ear that a good scrubbing won't cure.'

'If you can't see anything, hadn't you better keep me –'

'Keep you here so you can pester me?' snapped Father Simeon. He clicked his tongue impatiently. 'What job are you so anxious to shirk on a cold winter's day? Gardening?'

'Oh, no, I'm the keeper of the chalices now. I'm in charge of the wine and wafers for High Mass. It only takes up the mornings.'

'Well, you'd better hurry back to keeping the chalices, hadn't you?' replied Father Simeon coldly, picking up the pincers again. Brother Gilbert fled, catching the loose pocket of his habit on the latch in his haste to escape.

The smell of the young monk lingered in the room. As Father Simeon opened the door to let in some fresher air, he noticed something white on the ground. He crouched down with a crackle of knees. There was something wedged between the floor and the bottom edge of the oak door. He picked it up gently between his thumb and forefinger. It was a small circular piece of holy bread, just like the bread used at High Mass.

Father Simeon shuddered in horror, crossing himself hastily. He must have a word with the abbot about Brother Gilbert – too irresponsible to be entrusted with keeping the sacred chalices! He raised the wafer to his nose and sniffed three times, his nostrils flaring slightly to get a better scent.

'Curious!'

He frowned and sniffed again.

'A most unpleasant young man,' he muttered to himself, as he scurried along the corridor to Charlie's sickroom, 'and perhaps a little careless too!'

'Thank the Lord you are making a good recovery,' smiled Father Simeon, closing the lattice shutters and lighting some beeswax candles. 'I saw the improvement as soon as I gave you the milk-thistle cordial and applied the roasted-viper paste.'

Charlie was sitting in a chair close to the fire covered in sheepskins, his eyes huge in his pale face.

'I have ordered some strengthening food for you, but not from the castle kitchens. That old villain Sturgeon was trying to poison you, I have no doubt about it. He's been tried by ordeal and found guilty – red-hot irons, I'm told.'

'But Erik is still on the loose and, who knows, Sturgeon may have other accomplices in the kitchens besides him,' said Charlie shakily.

'Good heavens!' exploded Father Simeon, bending down stiffly to seize a black cat by the scruff of its neck and dump it out of the door. 'That is the third time I have caught that animal trying to slink into this room, the mangy beast. Now, Charlie,' he said confidentially, pulling up a stool. 'Marian tells me you and I have something in common – you're a bit of a herbalist yourself, I understand. Tell me, how did you stumble across the idea of toadstool poisoning? I must confess I was at a loss to understand what could be wrong with our poor novices. Was it just a clever guess, my dear?'

'We found it in a book. We were looking up the symptoms

suffered by the novices. It all seemed to fit – the drowsiness and the numbness in the limbs. And then we found a patch of death cap toadstools in the herb garden, and somebody had been collecting them on the night of the full moon. We'd even discovered a deadly poison that caused an itchy rash – we'd decided that poor Brother Harold died of that!'

Father Simeon snorted. 'We don't need reminding of that one, do we Charlie? Thank heavens for roasted vipers, eh? You had a lucky escape there.'

'I certainly did, Father Simeon!' said Charlie gratefully. 'But I still don't understand why Sturgeon killed Brother Harold. Why did he use something different that night? He was getting the result he wanted using toadstools.'

'Maybe he didn't intend to kill poor Brother Harold,' mused Father Simeon, scratching his head. 'Toadstools are pretty scarce when the weather turns cold. Perhaps he'd run out at the time and knew that mouldy rye produced a similar result and was as shocked as anyone when the poor boy died.'

'Yes,' said Charlie swallowing hard. 'But when he came to wanting to get rid of me, he knew exactly how deadly that poison could be!'

Father Simeon was fidgeting – pulling at the skin on his scrawny neck; a habit he had when worrying about something. 'But what I don't understand,' he said slowly, 'is how the novices were drugged. They all eat together in the refectory and their food is ladled from a single serving bowl. If poison had been slipped into the novices' food, why didn't it affect them all? Why only the ones guarding the book on any particular night?'

'Well, it's obvious, isn't it, Father Simeon?' said Charlie reflectively. 'It must be some food only those novices ate; something different from the ordinary refectory fare.'

Father Simeon's eyes widened. He sprang up suddenly, clutching Charlie's hand.

'You are a genius, my child! An absolute genius!' he cried in agitation. 'I must leave you alone for a while and make some investigations. I see it all clearly now. The novices did indeed eat something nobody else ate. But it was not in the refectory. Oh, dear me, no!' he exclaimed, whirling out of the room.

32
The Twisted Knife

Marian pinched her hood around her face as she hurried towards the infirmary, clutching the volume of Latin poems she'd borrowed for Charlie. She glanced up at the darkening sky, white gulls riding the currents. A sleety rain was falling, but a friendly glimmer of candlelight shone from Charlie's little room. A shadow passed swiftly in front of the lattice screen. Probably Father Simeon, she thought fondly, as another hurried shape crossed the opening. Marian frowned irritably. Charlie must have a lot of visitors this evening, and she really wanted some time with him alone.

Suddenly something thumped against the shutters with a dull thud. A shape lurched back, arm raised. Marian froze, snatching her breath. Only a few anxious seconds passed before two hooded forms emerged from the infirmary, struggling with a bulky sack. Marian shrank back silently into the shadow of the cloister wall, biting her hand to stifle a scream. She could hear muffled cries from inside the bag as the figures swiftly skirted the infirmary wall and hurried off in the direction of the cliff-top path.

Marian dropped the book with a cry and started to run towards the infirmary door. She stopped suddenly, gazing indecisively after the rapidly dwindling figures and then back towards the empty window. Then, with a sob of exasperation, she raced off after them into the murky dusk.

In the gloomy vestry Father Simeon knew exactly what he was looking for. It must be over fifty years ago that he had held the office of keeper of the chalices, but it seemed like only yesterday. Purposefully, he crossed to the wall cupboard and began to feel swiftly along the carved pattern of acorns running along its base. One, two, three acorns in from the left ... that should do it. He twisted the wooden nut. There was a soft click as the bolt shot back. He pulled open the cupboard cautiously to reveal the two golden chalices, bright enamelled colours glowing dimly in the half-light. As he felt along the top shelf his hand met a small wooden box full of wafers of holy bread. Moving down to the shelf below, his fingers jarred against a small bottle. He extracted the bung, raised it to his nose and sniffed deeply, his thin nostrils flaring. The odour was unmistakable. Years of working with herbs and plants had given him a nose as keen as any bloodhound. It was the same smell that he had noticed on the wafer that had fallen out of Brother Gilbert's pocket when he'd snagged it on the door!

'I thought as much,' breathed Father Simeon excitedly. '*Amanita phalloides* – the juice of the death cap!'

Father Simeon's gnarled old hands trembled as he replaced the bottle. He lifted the lid of the box of holy wafers and extracted a small flat circle of bread. Just as he expected – that telltale smell again. So this is how the novices were drugged! How simple for the keeper of the chalices to arrange it all! he mused grimly. All Brother Gilbert would need to know was which novice was to be guarding the Book. He could easily be slipped a poisoned wafer at mass that evening! Indignation welled up inside him. How dare Brother Gilbert defile this holy place with his poisonous brew? And where was the rogue now? Father Simeon's heart leapt as he remembered that he had left Charlie quite alone!

The old infirmarian raced across the frozen cloisters, skidding on the icy grass. The door to Charlie's room was ajar, but Father Simeon wrenched at the latch as if he were breaking into a locked room. Charlie's chair was quite empty. An overturned stool and some scuffle marks in the rushes by the hearthside indicated a struggle. Father Simeon let out a shriek.

'Great heavens! It is just as I feared! What a silly old fool I've been!'

Marian followed at a safe distance, keeping the hooded figures in view as they struggled with their bundle down the cliff-top path. I should have run for help after all, she thought in panic, but then I would have lost sight of where they were taking Charlie! In an agony of indecision, Marian tagged along, ducking behind boulders and shrinking behind scrubby bushes every time the kidnappers looked back to check they were not pursued. Reassured, they battled on, down the slippery ledges slick with rain, and into the hermit's lair. Marian crept down after them, her face red and smarting with wind, rain and tears.

Hovering uncertainly at the mouth of the cave, she could hear hurried exchanges coming from within. And then the muffled voices grew louder. 'God in heaven!' she breathed. 'They're coming out!' Trembling, Marian pressed her back into a hollow in the rough cliff face, praying that they wouldn't glance her way. She stifled a gasp of recognition when the wind caught Brother Gilbert's hood, as the cloaked forms passed within a hair's breadth of her, and began to scramble back up the cliff side. In an instant, Marian was inside the cave. The lumpy hessian sack lay on the stony floor where the scoundrels had dumped it, close to the entrance.

'Charlie!' she sobbed, fumbling with the drawstring, relieved to hear a strangled groan from within its folds. 'Are you all right? Thank heavens I saw them come for you!'

Charlie wriggled out of the sack, his face grey with pain.

'Ugh, you do look green,' said Marian, struggling to undo the greasy gag that cut into his mouth. 'What on earth was Brother Gilbert doing here? And who was the other one?'

'Erik!' replied Charlie grimly. 'They attacked me in the infirmary. I didn't have the strength to fight them. I cried for help but nobody came.'

'We've got get you out of here! They could be back at any minute,' she whispered urgently.

'I don't know if I can make it, Marian … I feel so weak!' Charlie's eyelids had begun to droop. He was failing fast.

'You must try, Charlie. They're sure to be back soon!'

'I'll do my best, Marian,' he mumbled faintly.

'Come on, then! Try to stand up,' she urged.

But she may as well have saved her breath. Charlie was only half conscious, slumped against her like a sack of grain.

'Charlie! Wake up!' she groaned, shaking him violently, unaware of the hermit who was creeping up stealthily from behind. Her moan of despair became a scream of terror as his withered old hand snaked around her neck and placed a twisted knife softly against her throat.

'Who are you? Reveal yourself, stranger!' croaked the hermit, sniffing the air. He wagged his head from side to side, alert and calculating. 'But wait!' he snarled. 'You've been here before! I've smelt you before! You're the thief who stole my apples!'

The hermit's bony fingers held her in an iron grip. She could feel the cold blade of the knife against her neck, smell the staleness of his unwashed body, the fetid stink of his breath. Marian dared not flinch. The hermit's curling toenails made a scuffing sound in the sand, like some monstrous bird of prey, as he dragged her towards his inner lair, leaving Charlie's unconscious body behind at the mouth of the outer cave.

Marian could hardly breathe. Come on, she told herself, he's only a frail old man! Closing her eyes tightly she summoned up all her courage, fighting down a wave of revulsion as she opened her mouth wide and sank her sharp teeth as hard as she could into his skinny arm. The old man screamed in fury. His bony fingers flew open and the knife thudded into the soft sand. Grasping her chance, she seized him by his puny shoulders and wrestled him to the floor, falling upon his shrunken body and pinning him to the ground.

The old man was winded, caught off guard, but now he fought back with the strength of a man three times his size. He clawed at her face with his talons, scoring red weals across her forehead and down her cheeks. Marian let go with a yelp and clutched at her bleeding face. At once he was upon her again, biting and scratching, pummelling her with his sharp fists, but Marian was younger and fitter. At last she had him vanquished on the floor, breathless and whimpering. Marian was taking no chances this time. A coiled rope lay by the fireside, just out of her reach.

'Charlie! Charlie,' she called hopelessly into the darkness. 'Come and help me! Just make one last effort and then you can rest again. Charlie! Please!'

She had her knee on the hermit's chest pressing down with all her weight. How long could she keep this up? At last she heard a sound coming from the mouth of the cave.

'Quick, Charlie. There's a rope. For heaven's sake, hurry!'

The hermit snarled fiercely, writhing in the dirt. She sensed his strength returning and was terrified he would surprise her again by springing up with a second wind.

'For pity's sake, Charlie, I know you're doing your best but –'

'Not so fast, Lady Marian!'

Marian drew back in terror, her mouth wide open in a silent scream. The firelight glinted on a meat cleaver, as Eadgyth raised the weapon high above her head. A drop of something warm dribbled down the blade, splashing on to Marian's robe, staining her yellow gown red.

33
Invisible Ink

The door of Abbot Gregory's study flew open. Father Simeon stood panting, wild eyed on the threshold.

'What in heaven's name is wrong, Simeon?' cried the abbot in alarm, setting down his quill pen. 'You look as if you have seen a ghost!'

'It's the boy, Abbot! He's ... he's disappeared,' gabbled Father Simeon. 'I only left him for a moment. You see, I had an idea ... I needed to investigate ... oh, why did I leave him alone!'

'Pray compose yourself, Simeon,' soothed the abbot, striding over to the old man and leading him to a chair in front of the fire. 'You will give yourself a seizure!'

Father Simeon half sat down and then immediately sprang up again.

'I ... I can't sit down ... I ... I must ... oh, Abbot, it is a matter of life and death ... I don't know how to break the news but ... Brother Gilbert ... the keeper of the chalices –'

'Take a deep breath and start at the beginning,'

commanded the abbot, pressing Father Simeon back down into his chair. 'Come, take some ale. I was planning to have some when Father Bernard joined me. I am expecting him at any moment with news of his investigations among the ancient volumes.'

Father Bernard changed his fur-lined slippers for his sturdy overshoes and picked up the candle from his cluttered writing desk. He was feeling low. How unbelievably unlucky! To have almost found a recipe for songbird pie and then to find it had been thrown away.

'Abbot Gregory will be disappointed,' he sighed as he emerged from his warm study into the freezing corridor. The candle flame lurched in an icy draught and Father Bernard cupped it in his hand to keep it alight. He stopped for a moment to listen. Somebody was running in the passageway. He sniffed impatiently. How many times must he ask the novices not to run in the monastery?

'Father Bernard, Father Bernard,' came a breathless voice from around the bend in the stairs. 'Oh, thank goodness! I've found you.'

Father Bernard recognized the plump-faced novice from the cellar of the ancient volumes. 'I … I thought I'd thrown it away,' he panted. 'You know, that recipe you wanted for songbird pie, but I rummaged in the rubbish and …'

He held out a crumpled piece of parchment, scorched and badly stained with mildew. Father Bernard's hand trembled as he took the cracked old vellum.

'Is it what you were looking for, Father?' asked the novice eagerly. He stared expectantly at Father Bernard as he studied the faded writing closely. The librarian shook his head sadly.

'Thank you for your trouble, my child, but this isn't going to help us after all. It is only a list of ingredients, nothing more,' he said. The novice looked dejected. 'I'll take it anyway,' he smiled kindly, pushing the parchment into the folds of his cloak. 'Saint Oswald is leading us all a merry dance, God rest his soul!' he sighed, as he made his way along the passage towards the abbot's room.

No sooner had Father Bernard crossed the threshold of the book-lined study, than he was bombarded by Father Simeon with the news of Charlie's disappearance and the enormity of the accusations against one of their own brother monks.

'So where is the treacherous Brother Gilbert now?' exploded Father Bernard. 'Are you convinced he has the boy with him? Does he have any idea that he is under suspicion?'

'I feel sure that Brother Gilbert did not feel the eye of suspicion upon him,' said Father Simeon contemptuously. 'If he had done so, he would not have come to the infirmary in such an impertinent fashion, asking questions about the boy.'

'Has anyone launched a search for the child?' demanded Father Bernard. 'Has there been any news?'

'We have dispatched the castle guards to comb the monastery and the fortress,' replied the abbot, 'but any hope of finding Brother Gilbert is fading fast. There is no trace of the wretch, but I am sure that Charlie must be with him. There were signs of a struggle in his room when Simeon reached it. The boy was as weak as a lamb;

it would have taken no great strength to overpower him.'

'But what is to be done about Charlie?' cried Father Bernard. 'Can we send out some strong young monks to aid in the search?'

'I do not think that would help, Bernard,' said Abbot Gregory. 'The castle guards are far better equipped to deal with a crisis such as this than we monks. Do not forget – they are armed!'

Father Bernard heaved a worried sigh. 'There are so many things that we do not understand. I cannot fathom the connection between one of our own brothers and Sturgeon in the kitchens! How did Brother Gilbert come to be involved in all this? What's the matter, Simeon? You look distracted.'

Father Simeon was taking short shallow breaths, almost as if he were sniffing for something, a puzzled expression on his face.

'Oh, nothing … I just … oh, probably nothing,' mumbled Father Simeon with an anxious frown.

'So, Bernard,' said the abbot, turning his attention to the librarian. 'Forgive me. Events in the infirmary have overtaken us. What news? Did you search the ancient volumes? Did you find any recipes?'

'Oh, there's nothing to report there, I'm afraid. I did find a recipe for songbird pie, but it turned out to be just a list of ingredients – nothing more.'

He rummaged in his cloak for the fragile old parchment that the novice had handed to him on the stairs.

'As I told you – merely a list of ingredients,' he said, handing it to the abbot.

Abbot Gregory took the proffered parchment and held it up close to the candle flame. 'Father Simeon, please light some more candles – it is so dark in here,' said the abbot. 'Simeon, did you hear me?'

Father Simeon was sniffing again, alert and listening, with a perplexed frown on his face.

'What is the matter with you tonight, Simeon? Your mind is wandering and yet we are discussing matters of the utmost importance,' snapped the abbot impatiently.

'I'm so sorry, Abbot,' apologized Simeon distractedly. 'What did you ask me to do?'

'Never mind the candles,' gasped Abbot Gregory, gazing incredulously at Father Bernard. 'What do you mean you found nothing of consequence? Are you quite mad, Bernard?'

'No, Abbot! I do not think I have taken leave of my senses quite yet,' said Father Bernard tartly. 'What do you mean?'

'Just a list, did you say? How can you have been so blind? Unless my eyes are deceiving me, you have handed me a map!'

More candles were hastily lit and soon the old monks were intent upon the fragile parchment spread out in the centre of the table.

'This is most curious,' said Father Bernard. 'I swear that there was no map on this page when I first examined it. It must have been the heat of the candle flame against the parchment that has developed these images!'

The drawing was faint and scarcely legible but Father

Simeon was sure that it was a map of the coastline just below the monastery. A church had been sketched on a large island in the far left-hand corner of the map. A further group of islands and rocks peppered the right-hand side of the parchment. A crude attempt to draw waves convinced him that the rocky outcrops were supposed to represent a group of islands that lay off the coast only a short distance from the shore.

'It is unmistakable,' said Father Simeon. 'I fished these waters as a boy and every island is known to me. There must be about thirty in all.'

'Yes,' added Father Bernard excitedly, 'and there is one large island with a building on it, and that is Saint Aidan's Isle. I am sure that this dark cross on the outlying island indicates the ancient ruined chapel that stands there still.'

'And what are these words written faintly alongside the cross on the map? They are too small for my dim eyes to see,' said Father Simeon.

Father Bernard peered at the map in the flickering light. '"*Thesaurus celatus est*" – The treasure is hidden here!' he exclaimed, translating the Latin. 'So the treasure lies on the island on which the ruined chapel of Saint Aidan still stands – hidden somewhere in that building, I shouldn't wonder! Someone must have foreseen that the northern raiders were coming all those years ago, and planned well in advance to hide the holy treasures.'

'It is clear what you must do,' announced Abbot Gregory, taking charge. 'You must set off at first light to the islands –'

'But what about Charlie?' interrupted Father Simeon anxiously. 'Aren't we forgetting –'

'The castle guards have been dispatched, Simeon. There is nothing more we can do for him at the moment. Let each man perform the task that God has given him. Leave the guards to do their work and let us do ours. Now, nobody knows about this map but we three. With good fortune the storm will have blown itself out by morning, and perhaps by then the search of the monastery and the castle will have revealed some clues as to the whereabouts of the boy. And now, my friends, it is time for High Mass. It is our duty to pray for the safety of the missing child.'

Father Bernard followed the abbot through the door and down the stone steps, but Father Simeon hung back. He seemed unwilling to leave the abbot's study. There must be more they could do to help poor Charlie, and there was something else bothering him. He stood hesitating at the top of the stairs, sniffing – that familiar smell again! Then, shrugging his shoulders in exasperation, he followed his companions down the stairs.

No sooner had the solid oak door banged shut than Brother Gilbert scrambled out of the iron-bound chest in which he had been hiding. He waited barely a minute after he had seen the last black-habited figure disappear around the turning on the stairs before he began to tiptoe in the opposite direction. Within minutes he was out in the herb garden. Pausing in the shadow of the abbey, he cupped his hands around his mouth and gave a cry like a screech owl. On the third call another scrawny figure dressed in scullions' white emerged from the kitchen yard to join him. A hurried conversation and then they were off, weaving like hares between the scrubby bushes which lined the track leading away from the monastery towards the cliff top, and from there down the slippery zigzag path towards the beach.

The three elderly monks trudged in gloomy silence towards the chapel.

'Hurry, Simeon,' called Abbot Gregory over his shoulder. 'What is wrong with Simeon this evening?' he grumbled to Father Bernard.

'He has taken the news of the boy very hard, Abbot,' replied Father Bernard, turning sharply as Father Simeon cried out from behind. 'What is it now, Simeon?'

'God forgive me for being such a fool!' he cried. 'I couldn't place the foul stench and yet we were talking about the villain even as I struggled to identify it!'

'Stench? What stench do you mean?' said Father Bernard.

'Brother Gilbert! I knew I recognized that smell in your study as soon as I entered. I am sorry to have to tell you, Abbot, but Brother Gilbert was there in your room while we were discussing the map and the treasure!'

'But where could he have been hiding?'

'I do not pretend to know where he had concealed his villainous body, but he was there – I would stake my life on it! He must have overheard every word.'

The abbot's eyes widened. 'This news has changed everything! We cannot leave our task until morning. Father Bernard! You are excused from High Mass. Fetch some implements from the kitchen garden – a spade, an axe and anything else you can find, and make haste to the boathouse! Father Simeon! Choose a trusty young monk to help with the rowing and take him down to join Bernard on the beach. I must attend to High Mass and then remain behind to await developments. I cannot leave the monastery at a time like this. And Simeon – you must stay with me. You are too frail to make this journey.'

'I will fetch Brother Dominic from the infirmary at once, Abbot,' replied Father Simeon huffily, 'but if you think Bernard is leaving me behind just because I am over ninety years old, then you are badly mistaken!'

34
A Family Affair

Marian shrank back from Eadgyth, eyes tight shut, waiting for the blow. Nothing came. Why didn't she strike and end the agony of waiting?

'Who's there?' rapped the cook sharply. Something had distracted her, staying her arm in mid-air, the cleaver poised above Marian's head.

'It's only the storm, Eadgyth … only the wind,' wheezed the hermit, pushing Marian off and scrambling out from under her. 'You came just in time!'

'Silence, fool! I can hear footsteps. Hold the girl!' She cocked her head, listening intently while the hermit secured Marian's wrists and ankles. She dared not struggle, with Eadgyth towering over her clutching the bloodstained cleaver. A filthy rag stuffed into her mouth soon stopped her moans. Marian watched in horror as Brother Gilbert and Erik shuffled into the firelight, dragging the still body of Charlie behind them, leaving a trail of blood in the sand. Eadgyth let the cleaver fall to her side.

'You should have called out,' she snapped. 'I thought we were discovered.'

'Best not leave this outside,' laughed Erik, flinging Charlie to the floor. 'Might just give the game away!'

'What news, Gilbert?' said Eadgyth with a frown. 'Are they searching for the boy?'

'They have searched in vain, cousin,' sneered Brother Gilbert, flashing a poisonous glance at Charlie.

'He died without a murmur!' muttered Eadgyth grimly.

'And he's not the only one out of harm's way now,' mocked Brother Gilbert, inclining his head towards Marian. 'Well done, cousin.'

'Oh, excuse me, Lady Marian,' smirked Eadgyth spitefully. 'I was forgetting my manners. Let me introduce our visitors. I think you've already met my uncle,' she crowed, waving the bloody weapon towards the hermit, 'and this is Brother Gilbert, my cousin from the monastery, and Erik, my little brother! A family affair you might say – the affair of the lawful heirs to Goslar Castle. Your scheming ancestor Sven the Guzzlar took this castle from my family. Well, it's our turn now. We mean to find the treasure what's rightfully ours – taken from us all those years ago by you greedy Goslars!'

She kicked Marian cruelly on her shin. Marian turned her head away. She couldn't bear to look at Charlie's lifeless body.

'Oooh, an' I was forgettin'. You an' Erik's got a lot in common,' she taunted. 'Both great friends of Charlie Ferret, I understand – and you can stop that moaning.'

'Yeah,' sneered Erik. 'Pity it all went wrong – we was

such close friends, me and Charlie … and you was fond of him too, weren't you, Eadgyth? Until he got above himself …'

'He got what he deserved!' she snapped venomously. 'I was good to him and just look how he repaid my kindness! Never does no good to start prying into other people's business, young lady. But you weren't no good at it, were you?' she sniped, prodding Marian again with her boot.

'Oh, yes, Lady Marian,' sneered Erik. 'I saw you both spying on Eadgyth that night in the garden. And I saw our "clever herbalist" looking up toadstools in that book of his! Too smart for 'is own good, your friend, Charlie – thought he could frighten Eadgyth – leaving a poisonous toadstool in her basket of goose eggs. That was a big mistake! There was only one thing for it after that, wasn't there, Eadgyth?'

'Afraid so, Erik,' said Eadgyth in mock sorrow. 'You had to give 'im a little push, didn't you?'

'Yeah,' swanked Erik. 'And I even fooled those doddering old monks into blaming old Sturgeon! That's the best joke of all! Couldn't have been easier – planting them toadstools in 'is spice store and telling them monks Sturgeon was the poisoner!'

Marian groaned, struggling against the gag. So Sturgeon was innocent after all! They'd arrested the wrong person! But it was too late now. Charlie was dead and there was no way she could tell anyone the truth.

'That's enough boasting now, Erik,' barked Eadgyth impatiently. 'You made a bit of a mess of it yerself, if the truth be known! You didn't push him hard enough, did you? Caused a lot of extra bother for me. I had to send over them rye cakes – get rid of 'im that way!'

'Look who's bragging now!' sulked Erik. 'That didn't work neither, did it? Me an' Gilbert had to go and risk our necks in the infirmary! We might have been spotted and then what?'

'That's enough, Erik!' snapped Eadgyth. 'What does it matter now? I've dealt him the final blow and the girl will soon follow! That is the end of the evidence against us as far as the poisoning is concerned, but we are still no nearer to finding the treasure.'

'Ah, but that's where you're wrong, cousin!' cut in Brother Gilbert, looking smug. 'You're so busy bickering among yourselves – nobody's asked me why I've come. I've some very interesting news for you, but if you prefer to squabble like children …' He turned as if to leave.

'You have discovered something?' said Eadgyth eagerly. 'Tell me at once!'

'Your quest is over, sweet cousin,' he announced in triumph. 'I have discovered where the treasure lies hidden!'

'Where?' cried Eadgyth, springing towards him. 'If you know where the treasure is, go and fetch it for me. I insist you go now!'

Brother Gilbert held up a restraining hand.

'I have discovered that the treasure is buried on Saint Aidan's Isle. I overheard the Fathers talking in the library earlier today. I knew they were on to something, so I kept my eyes and ears open.' He lowered his voice. 'Our only hope is this. I do not believe the monks intend to set out tonight. The weather is too stormy and they do not think there is any need to hurry. If we set sail now, we will have at least a twelve-hour start on them.'

'What are we waiting for, then?' cried Eadgyth, her eyes glittering. 'Let's launch the boats. Erik – you bundle that boy into a rowing boat and set off at once. Give the brat a watery grave and then make haste to meet us on the island. We'll need more than one boat to load all the booty! Gilbert an' me'll follow you in another boat when we've gathered lanterns and spades together. Gilbert – you go and help Erik load the body and then come back and help me with the gear.'

'Take care nobody sees you, boys,' croaked the hermit, as they hauled Charlie out of the cave by his heels.

Unnoticed, Balthazar crept after them, pressing close into the shadow of the wall.

'And now, my precious one,' grinned the hermit, turning to Eadgyth. 'What shall we do with the girl while you're away?'

'Finish her off now, Uncle!' she cried, lunging for the cleaver. 'Then there's no one left to betray us.'

'Not so hasty, my impetuous one. Do you not think Lady Marian could be more useful to us alive than dead – at least for the moment? I trust that you will arrive in advance of the monks, but what if you are pursued? Lady Marian may be a useful hostage. We would do well to keep her alive, at least for a little while longer.'

'You may have a point, Uncle,' said Eadgyth reluctantly. 'If anything goes wrong we can use the girl to bargain with. We can silence her later when we know that all is well.' She ran her finger ominously across her throat.

'Exactly so. Leave her in the tender hands of Uncle. Don't you worry about us,' he grinned, poking Marian with his grimy toes. 'We can tell each other stories by the fireside until you get back with the treasure, can't we, my dear?'

'Well, be sure she's securely bound,' snapped Eadgyth, coiling some rope around her forearm. 'She must not escape and sound the alarm. Now, where are them lanterns? Oooh, why doesn't Gilbert hurry up?' She stamped her foot in irritation.

Brother Gilbert stumbled back into the cave, clutching a stitch in his side.

'You took your time,' complained Eadgyth.

'That boy was heavier than he looked and it's a long way down to the beach,' he panted. 'Give me a minute to catch my breath and then we'll be on our way.'

Eadgyth was ready to go, standing in the middle of a pile of spades and lanterns, her skirts hitched up around her stocky thighs, ready for the climb down to the beach.

'We can't take that lot, Eadgyth!' puffed Brother Gilbert. 'How can we carry it all? Just a couple of lanterns and a spade will have to do.'

'Aren't you forgetting something important?' croaked the hermit, as Eadgyth impatiently shouldered the spade. She rounded angrily on the old man, and then her eyes lit up when she saw what he held in his hand.

'You always were good to me, Uncle,' she smiled grimly, snatching up the twisted knife.

Erik's lonely lantern swung over the heaving sea. He paused in his rowing for a moment, the oily black water swirling around the resting oars, and gazed at Charlie's motionless form and then out into the vast, desolate ocean. Balthazar closed his green eyes tightly, a dark shape, curled in behind a coil of rope in the bow, biding his time. A gust of wind blew spray, like sharp stones, in Erik's face. His cockiness was rapidly turning into panic, alone with a corpse and the wind rising. He suddenly felt vulnerable, small and lost. He began to babble to calm himself.

'I was wonderin' if you could do anything about my ingrowing toenails,' he mocked, with more bravado than he felt.

The boat rocked unsteadily as a flash of lightning glowed white against Charlie's bloodstained tunic.

'What – you can't do nothing for them? I thought you was supposed to be a healer,' he blustered, wiping the spray out of his stinging eyes with his sleeve. 'If you tell me what herbs you need, I'll go and fetch 'em from the kitchen garden.' He pulled on the oars and stopped again in mid-stroke. ''Ere, how's that friend of yours – Lady Marian Goslar? Ha ha ha! Ooh, a bit tied up at the moment, is she? Geddit – a bit tied up? Ooh, that reminds me, I'd better tie this anchor around your ankles before I chuck you over.' He gazed anxiously across the wildly churning waters, grey sheets of rain driving across the sky. 'I wonder if Eadgyth and Gilbert have set off yet. I'd better not be too long. I don't want them getting there first and taking all the best treasure for themselves now, do I?'

Unnoticed by Erik, Charlie was stirring in the bottom of the boat. The heaving of the sea, the freezing water on his face, and the brutal kicks from Erik's stout boots had roused him. The salt water stung his bruised lips and the biting wind sliced through his thin scullion's clothes. Charlie strained his ears to hear Erik's ramblings, too dazed to make much sense of them. It seemed that someone was planning to throw him over the side. He didn't much care. But something was tickling his face. He twitched violently, but Erik was hunched over the oars, absorbed in the rowing. The tickling sensation came again, followed by Balthazar's fishy breath on his face. Charlie could feel a sneeze gathering at the back of his nose.

'A … a … a … tishooo!'

Erik screeched, dropping the oars in terror.

'God's death! What the devil?' His heart was thundering with the rising wind. 'Y … y … you not dead?' he stammered in disbelief. 'C … c … course you are. You must be!' he gabbled. 'Eadgyth hit you with the cleaver!'

Balthazar was crouching low in the bottom of the boat just at Charlie's head.

'Rouse yourself, Charlie,' he urged. 'Gather all your strength. Make an effort! Heaven knows, I am. Surely you know how much cats hate water!'

'What in the name of hell are you?' gibbered Erik, staring in horror at Charlie's stirring body. 'A ghoul? A spectre?'

Charlie groaned. He was fully conscious now.

Erik, quaking and blubbering with fear, rose unsteadily to his feet, the small craft lurching on the waves. He was terrified, alone on the vast empty sea with only a spectre for company! He grabbed an oar, swung it back, preparing to lunge with all his strength at Charlie in the bottom of the boat.

But Balthazar pounced faster! Spitting and snarling like a fiend from hell, he punched his outstretched claws into Erik's back, puncturing his flesh, clawing his hair, biting his shoulders and neck. Erik turned round and round in the boat, arms flailing, trying to see what was behind him, but Balthazar clung tight, ducking this way and that to avoid Erik's whirling arms.

Erik was howling now, calling in vain for his friends to help him. Charlie had hauled himself up on to his knees and was staring in bewilderment at Erik writhing in panic, Balthazar clinging to his neck.

'Help, Charlie! Help!' cried Erik. 'There's a devil from hell on my back! Help! I'm your friend, remember. It was just a joke, Charlie, honest! I never meant to throw you overboard.'

Charlie's fever was raging. The world spun round and back again as he lay in the heaving boat. His eyes wouldn't focus. He could see three Eriks, four Eriks, merging back into one Erik. His trembling fingers travelled to his chest, groping for the cross. It felt different, he thought, vaguely puzzled. Rough and mangled – not as smooth as he remembered it. It must have taken the force of the blow when Eadgyth hit him with the cleaver.

'Rouse yourself, Charlie,' screamed Balthazar. 'I can't hold on for ever!'

But even as he yelled, a giant wave was gathering its strength. Convulsing the ocean, it slapped against the bow of the boat, sending the little craft spiralling out of control. With a scream of anguish, Erik lost his footing, reeled backwards in the boat and tripped over an abandoned oar.

He fell howling over the side, into the roiling waves.

'Heelp! I can't swim. Heelp!' screamed Erik, flailing in the water. A sudden gust of wind sent the boat spinning away from the thrashing body. For a moment Erik's head disappeared from view. 'Come back,' gurgled Erik, bobbing up again, only to be flung further away by a wave that split the sea.

Balthazar hauled himself up from where he had landed spreadeagled in the bottom of the boat.

'He would have killed you first, you know, Charlie,' he growled. He nudged Charlie's exhausted body firmly with his paw. 'Are you all right, Charlie? Can you hear me? Charlie! Speak to me!'

Charlie groaned. 'I ... I can't row us back, Balthazar. I ... I haven't the strength.'

'Well, that's just great! What am I supposed to do with you now? I should never have told your mother I'd look after you!' he grumbled, as the waves carried the small craft on towards the island.

35
Sheep's Ankle Bones

The sea was rough but the tide was in their favour as Eadgyth and Brother Gilbert scrambled into the boat. If they hurried, they could reach the island before the storm had risen to full strength. They hoisted up the small anchor and pulled away from the shore, Gilbert rowing, Eadgyth sitting in the prow.

'Just wait till I get my hands on them treasures,' she breathed, eyes glittering, 'and claim back what's rightly mine at last. All these years – slaving away in the kitchens serving them Guzzlars! But now it'll be me what's sitting around on cushions, gobbling pastries, but they won't be ones what I've made meself!'

'What the devil are you doing, Eadgyth?' shouted Gilbert above the noise of the sea. 'You'll tip us into the water!'

She'd staggered to her feet in the boat, her braided hair blown loose by the wind. 'I'll wear jewels and pearls and …'

The boat rocked dangerously, the lanterns casting crazy bobbing patterns on the seething water.

'If you don't sit down and keep still, you'll be wearing seaweed round your neck at the bottom of the ocean! You talk as if the treasure's all yours – this is a family affair, remember! Now, grab that paddle and give us a hand.'

She sat down at last with a grunt and concentrated on the task. Once started, Eadgyth paddled like a woman possessed. The waves grew higher as the little craft tossed and reared into the gathering night, its timbers creaking as the waves heaved it violently up and down. Lightning crackled across the blue-black sky as they laboured towards the speck of land that grew bigger as the skies darkened.

'Row, Gilbert, row! Put your back into it,' laughed Eadgyth, bailing the water out with a leather bucket. 'The wind's behind us, blowing us towards the island!'

The monks' stout boots crunched on the shingle as they struggled, ankle-deep in freezing seawater, to launch their sturdy fishing boat into the outgoing tide.

'Are you sure this is wise, Father Simeon?' said Brother Dominic in disgruntled tones, helping the old man unsteadily aboard, clutching a garden hoe. 'Surely nothing can be so urgent that it cannot wait until morning.'

'We will explain as we go. We need a strong young monk to help with the rowing and, God willing, maybe some digging too!'

'Make haste, Simeon, hand me up the lantern,' urged Father Bernard impatiently. 'Pull for the island. The tide is with us but the wind is high and the currents are treacherous.'

A sudden gust of wind flung seawater from the oars into their faces.

'You should not have come, Simeon,' said Father Bernard anxiously.

'I do wish you would stop treating me like an invalid,' snapped Father Simeon. 'I am barely thirty years your senior! Oh, I forgot.' He rummaged in his cloak pockets. 'Take these, all of you, and wear them around your necks. A sheep's ankle bone for everyone – an amulet against drowning.'

Father Bernard squeezed his arm. 'Bless you, Simeon. I don't know where we'd be without you.'

The small boat laboured slowly through the waves. Brother Dominic grunted as he pulled on the sturdy oars. It was hard going, and they had to keep a sharp lookout for hidden rocks.

'With the greatest respect, Father Simeon,' he puffed, 'would somebody mind telling me why we are here?'

Eadgyth and Brother Gilbert were already nearing the island.

'We'll need to find a secure spot for the boat,' puffed Gilbert. 'We don't want to get stranded on the island. Not with all the lovely treasure.'

'We'll have Erik's boat as well, don't forget. He should be here already. He was well ahead of us. You find a secure mooring. I'll jump out here,' said Eadgyth impatiently, as the hull of the boat scraped the shingle.

'Look out,' cried Father Simeon, squinting through the

stinging blur of rain as they steered between the rocks that scattered the shallows. The monks had had a rougher time of it, approaching the island from the south and making slower progress.

'Row, Brother Dominic! One last effort and we will feel the shingle beneath the hull,' cried Father Bernard.

Father Bernard was the first monk ashore, stumbling up the rocks and securing the boat, as Father Simeon, balancing with difficulty, held a lantern for him.

'Simeon, you stay behind and guard the boat while Brother Dominic and I investigate the chapel,' ordered Father Bernard. 'Dominic, you bring the spades; I will carry lanterns.'

'Great heavens, Bernard,' exploded Father Simeon. 'There you go again – treating me as if I am decrepit! I have not come all this way to be –'

'My dear Simeon,' said Father Bernard, holding up his hand to silence him. 'You are fortunate that I have allowed you to come at all. Now, accept your age for once and remain with the boat. Brother Dominic is young and strong. He will accompany me.'

Eadgyth and Brother Gilbert had already reached the chapel. They burst in through the rotten door.

'Hurry up, you fool,' snapped Eadgyth. 'Keep up, can't you? Hand me the spade.'

'Er … er … the spade, Eadgyth? I … I …'

She turned on him in fury.

'Don't tell me you left it behind! You'll have to go all the way back to the boat. It's taken us ages to scramble here over them slippery rocks, what with you skidding about in them flimsy sandals.'

'I'm s … sorry, Eadgyth,' he stammered. 'I … I put it down when I was helping you out of the boat. I'll go back and fetch it. I won't be long.'

'Oh, I'll go,' she snapped impatiently. 'I can get back quicker in these boots. I'll have a look for Erik on the way. He must have moored the boat by now. He's been ages and we need another pair of hands.'

Eadgyth stomped off to collect the spade from the northern shore, unnoticed by the monks who were approaching the chapel from the opposite side. On reaching the water she stared out to sea, searching for Erik and the boat. Ah, there it was, a small craft lurching towards the beach. She squinted into the driving rain. How very odd. It looked like Erik's boat, but there was no sign of Erik at the oars.

Up in the ruined chapel, Brother Gilbert set to work, unaware of the creeping monks edging stealthily up to the broken doorway. He lit a flaming brand from the lantern and began frantically scanning the damp walls for clues, a loose stone, any telltale sign of a hiding place for the lovely treasure. He grinned craftily. If only he could find it before Eadgyth came back!

'There's a light in the chapel,' whispered Father Bernard, clutching Brother Dominic's sleeve. 'The devils have beaten us to it! Tread carefully, they may well be armed.'

Brother Gilbert spun round at the sound of footsteps.

'You were quick, Eadgyth! You must have run fast. I can't seem to find … oh …' he stammered, caught off guard.

'F ... F ... Father Bernard!' An ingratiating smile hovered around the corners of his thin lips. 'B ... B ... Brother Dominic, th ... thank the Lord you are safe,' he faltered, as the two monks hurried into the chapel out of the stinging rain.

Gilbert's wily mind raced. This could ruin everything! He must be wary; play for time. Surely his fat cousin would be back with the spade before long – and where the devil was Erik?

'W ... word r ... reached the monastery that you had set sail in the storm,' he gabbled, glancing over his shoulder in agitation, 'and I c ... came to see if there was anything that I could do to help.'

Father Bernard's face was an inscrutable mask, immobile except for a tiny tic that twitched at the corner of his eye. 'And who, pray, informed you that help was needed?' he asked steadily.

'I ... c ... came as soon as I could ...' he grovelled, edging around Father Bernard and placing himself between the elderly priest and the ruined doorway.

Father Bernard gave an outraged snort, his face dark with anger.

'Did you indeed?' he replied evenly, his eyes like stones. 'And how, pray, did word reach the monastery? How came you to hear of our plight?'

The wind moaned in the ancient belfry and hail clattered like pebbles on the decaying roof of the chapel. The three monks eyed each other warily, tense nerves bristling.

I cannot guess how much they know, thought Brother Gilbert, his knuckles white around the flaming brand, but at least we will be evenly matched when Eadgyth returns.

All at once Father Bernard's eyes widened as he glimpsed a movement behind Brother Gilbert, beyond the crumbling arch of the doorway.

'You wicked scoundrel!' rapped Father Bernard suddenly. 'And you, one of our community's own brethren. How came your mind to be so polluted by the Devil?'

Brother Gilbert's sharp features glowed livid in the wavering lantern light, his obsequious expression fading as the ghastly truth sank in. Father Bernard might be a rheumatic old fool, he realized with rising panic, but Brother Dominic – that fit young monk is more than a match for me! He took a faltering step back then twitched in sudden relief at the crunch of Eadgyth's boots approaching from behind. He grinned in triumph as he heard a sharp intake of breath from Father Bernard. Slowly, inch by inch, he raised the flaming brand above his head.

'Let's finish them off, Eadgyth,' he cried, his cockiness returning as he lunged at the monks.

Too late! In a moment Gilbert was sprawling on the stony floor of the chapel, sparks flying from the fiery weapon as it flew out of his hands and skidded across the ground. He screamed in surprise and indignation as Brother Dominic sprang to the aid of old Father Simeon, who had crept up behind Brother Gilbert from the shadowy archway and seized him around the ankles.

'Secure the fiend!' cried Father Simeon, fumbling to unfasten his rope belt. 'Here, take this, Brother Dominic. Hurry now! Thank heavens I arrived in time!'

'God's blood! You saved our lives!' cried Father Bernard. 'This traitor would have put out our eyes with this flaming brand!' he said, picking up the smouldering branch.

'I thought you had taken leave of your senses, Father Bernard,' grunted Brother Dominic in relief as he bound Brother Gilbert's ankles with the belt. 'I had not noticed Father Simeon creeping in.'

'Let me go! Let me go!' whined Gilbert. 'What are you doing? This is outrageous. I'll report you to Abbot Gregory! I am keeper of the chalices, I'll have you know!'

'Well, what do you have to say now, Bernard?' grinned Father Simeon smugly, his sense of mischief overcoming his pique at being left behind. 'Hadn't you better send me back to guard the boat? I fear I am forgetting to remember my age! Or perhaps you are just a trifle pleased that my curiosity got the better of me!'

Alone on the beach, Eadgyth braced herself against the buffeting wind, thick legs planted in the sand. Wild hair whipped her face. She dashed away the rain from her smarting eyes and peered into the storm, watching the boiling sea driving the wayward boat towards the rocks.

'Erik,' she cried into the howling wind. 'Where in God's name are you? Erik! Don't go playin' games with me. We need your help to dig for the treasure. ERIK!'

Charlie crouched feverishly in the bottom of the boat, Balthazar beside him, quaking in terror.

'Hold on, Charlie! Brace yourself,' cried the cat. 'We're going to hit the rocks!'

Balthazar plummeted forward as the prow splintered

on the jagged granite, disgorged from the sea at last by a monstrous surging wave.

'Get up Charlie!' urged Balthazar. 'We've run aground! Get out now. It's our only chance. Any minute now we'll be washed out to sea again!'

Eadgyth had dropped the spade and begun to stumble towards the broken craft, skirts bunched in one hand, lantern held high in the other.

'Erik! Where are you?'

She sprang back with a strangled cry as Charlie rose like a spectre from the boat.

'What devilish horror is this?' she gibbered, her voice quaking. 'I … I thought you were dead … What are you? A g … ghost? … R … revenge from beyond the grave?'

Charlie staggered out of the boat, faint with nausea and pain. He reeled towards the stricken figure, barely recognizing the contorted face. He was disorientated, confused. Wasn't that Eadgyth? But what was she doing here and why was she so afraid of him?

'Get away from me, foul fiend from hell!' she screamed in panic, backing away from Charlie, but still unable to tear her terrified eyes away from his ashen face. Charlie could hear her harsh breathing, strangled moans and pitiful gasps of dread as she fumbled in her apron.

'Charlie, look out!' screeched Balthazar. 'She's got a knife!'

Charlie stumbled back with a whimper. The cold moonlight gleamed on the cruel blade. He glanced over his shoulder at the heaving water. With his back to the sea on the slippery rocks there was no escape! With a sickening lurch, his stomach seemed to fall away, and he knew that his time had come at last. Death had found him, on a windswept beach, lonely and far from home.

Then, just as the flame of his courage was flickering out, Charlie felt a familiar warmth under the thin fabric of his scullion's clothes, rising to a burning heat that made him cry out in surprise. The amber cross was burning on his chest, its strength surging through his veins, steadying his nerve. His fear became rage; his despair courage. Fever and pain were gone. His body bristled with renewed energy. He heard the words of Saint Oswald ringing in his ears. *Embrace your fear, my child!*

'Be gone, murderess!' he screamed in a voice not his own. 'Be gone, poisoner of innocent novices!' he roared.

Eadgyth's candle flared wildly inside the lantern. She leapt back with a groan, her petrified eyes locked on Charlie's. The twisted knife slipped through her trembling fingers and clattered to the ground.

'No,' she screeched, 'No! I never meant no harm! I never meant to kill you!'

For an instant she stood rooted to the spot, the lantern held high above her head, mouth slack, eyes wild and staring like some pitiful creature brought to bay by the hunt. And then, with a blood-curdling scream, she dropped the lantern with a crash and fled howling across the weed-strewn boulders, all thoughts of the treasure forgotten.

Charlie sank exhausted to the ground, the amber cross already scarcely warm on his chest. Balthazar crouched next to him, warming his face with his breath. Charlie's energy was spent, but the villain had fled, believing in her

wicked heart that he had come for her: a terrible visitation
– revenge from beyond the grave.

36
Saint Peter's Fingernails

'You must get up,' urged Balthazar, nudging Charlie with his paw. 'You can't just lie here in the middle of a storm!'

Charlie's feverish eyes glittered as a bolt of lightning rent the sky.

'I haven't saved you from Erik to watch you die on the beach,' he hissed, rubbing the side of his head against Charlie's cold, wet cheek. 'You're in grave danger. We have to find you some shelter.'

'But where can we go?' shivered Charlie in despair. 'The boat's smashed to pieces and the oars are gone.'

Balthazar sprang up on to an outcrop of rock, peering frantically into the distance, narrowing his eyes against the freezing rain. 'There's a light over there,' he said uncertainly, glancing desperately back at Charlie's hunched body. 'Look, Charlie. Do you see?' He darted back to Charlie's side, tugging urgently at his clothes.

'Perhaps it's Mother … out looking for me in the rain …'

mumbled Charlie.

Balthazar froze, searching his friend's face with intense green eyes. 'It's going to be all right, Charlie,' he growled, swallowing down a lump in his throat. 'I'm going ahead to investigate. Just you hold on until I get back.'

'Where's the boy, Brother Gilbert?' snarled Father Simeon, grabbing the trembling monk by the throat. 'We know that you took him from his room in the infirmary. I hurried back as soon as I had discovered your poisonous brew in the vestry, but I was already too late!'

'I ... I ... didn't ... I ... I don't know ...' stammered Brother Gilbert, squirming in the dirt of the chapel floor.

'Father Simeon,' rapped Father Bernard contemptuously. 'Put the wretch down. His mouth is full of lies and guile.'

'Then we must make him tell the truth, Bernard,' Father Simeon said, tightening his grip. 'Charlie was weak and ill before he disappeared from the infirmary. He may even now be beyond our help. I ask you again, Brother Gilbert. Where is the boy?'

'I'm here, Father Simeon,' croaked Charlie weakly from the doorway. He staggered drunkenly against the broken frame before slumping heavily to the ground, his bare hands and feet ragged from clawing up the rocks from the beach.

'Great heavens! It's Charlie!' gasped Father Simeon.

The Fathers stared at the boy in amazement. The light from Simeon's lantern glinted on the amber cross hanging around Charlie's neck. It lay on his chest, the gold twisted and mangled, the stone crushed as if from the blow of some heavy weapon. Following Simeon's gaze, Charlie clutched at the broken object where it lay directly above his heart.

'I think it saved my life,' he whispered. 'When Eadgyth hit me with the meat cleaver, it took the full force of the blow.'

'Eadgyth? Who is Eadgyth?' asked Father Bernard, puzzled.

'Oh, never mind that now,' fussed Father Simeon, rummaging in his cloak. 'Do you not see the child is fearfully wounded? Now, I'm sure I brought some wolfbane with me. Ah, here we are,' he smiled, drawing a cloudy bottle from the folds of his cloak. 'It will tingle a little at first, but a dulling of the pain soon follows.'

'What do we do now, Simeon?' asked Father Bernard anxiously. 'We cannot attempt to take the boy back until the tide has turned. It would be much too perilous!'

'Er ... if I might make a suggestion, Father,' ventured Brother Dominic hesitantly.

'Of course, my child,' said Father Bernard.

'Well, as we can't row home against the tide,' said Brother Dominic, flexing his strong arms, 'don't you think we might as well start digging?'

Father Bernard gazed doubtfully around at the empty walls of the ruined chapel. 'It is a fine idea, Dominic,' he agreed, perplexed, 'but I cannot see any obvious hiding place unless ...' He followed Brother Dominic's gaze as it came to rest on Charlie, slumped down on a dark granite slab in the centre of the rough earth floor. His eyes lit up. 'Shoulder the spade, Brother Dominic! Come, Father Simeon! Let us discover what lies beneath this stone.'

Charlie's eyes glittered with fever as he watched the monks scrabbling in the earth with hands and spades. He was dozing fitfully, propped against the chapel wall. Balthazar sat trembling in the shadows, teeth chattering – a matted ball of sodden fur.

'Pull Dominic, pull with all your might,' wheezed Father Bernard, leaning into the granite slab. 'Mind your fingers, Simeon, this stone is as heavy as lead. Have a care. You are not as young as you were.'

The figures of the monks swam before Charlie's eyes. 'I don't know what's happened to Mother ...' he murmured, drifting back into uneasy sleep.

'Don't try to talk, my child,' puffed Father Simeon, glancing at him with a troubled frown. 'We need to get Charlie back to the infirmary, Bernard, just as soon as the tide has turned.'

The huge stone slab eased from the earth with a ripping sound as centuries of spiders' webs tore apart in a cloud of dust. A rotten putrid smell of damp and the mould of ages enveloped them. As the dust settled, the monks crouched in stunned silence, surveying the treasure. Fragments of fabric clung to the beautiful objects, hidden from human gaze for hundreds of years. Father Bernard knelt down by the musty trench, bowed his head for a few breaths before reaching out a trembling hand to touch a small golden box, embossed with a slim cross of lapis lazuli.

'Look, Charlie,' said Father Simeon excitedly. Charlie opened his sleepy eyes. Golden cups and fine silver plate lay in a gleaming pile.

'Who knows what these caskets may contain,' gasped Father Bernard in awe, meeting Charlie's befuddled gaze with tears in his eyes. 'The legendary finger of Saint Aidan, perhaps, or Saint Peter's fingernails. Imagine how the pilgrims will flock to the abbey!'

'Yes, Bernard,' said Father Simeon, dusting his hands on his habit. 'And to think that such rare and holy things might have fallen into the hands of a wretch like this!' He nodded towards Gilbert.

'Untie me now!' moaned the pitiful monk. 'There's a wild woman at large on this island who's dangerous and armed. It's her you should be tying up, not me!'

Father Bernard started in sudden alarm. 'Of course. What fools we are! There may be other villains abroad on this island with similar evil intent. Brother Dominic! Go and see if the tide has turned. Check on the boat! We must leave this desolate place as soon as ever we can.'

There was no more fitting punishment for Brother Gilbert than to have to lie tightly bound on the floor of the chapel, listening to the excited voices of the monks busily stacking the treasure by the chapel door. His greedy eyes flicked over the glittering mound of gold. At last they had finished.

'Where has Brother Dominic got to now?' puffed Father Bernard impatiently. 'I only sent him out to check on the tide.'

'I'm back, Father,' wheezed burly Brother Dominic, staggering into the church, carrying a shrieking bundle in his arms. 'I found this poor creature raving on the beach. I don't know who she is but I couldn't leave her there alone;

she was about to do herself an injury.'

The bundle was Eadgyth. At least, it looked like Eadgyth, except that her hair had turned completely white.

37
Razor Shells

Marian was alone. The hermit was nowhere to be seen. She held her breath and listened. There was no sound of his wheezy breathing. She must try to stay calm; quell the feeling of rising panic that threatened to suffocate her as she retched against the filthy gag. How could anybody save her from the evil old hermit when nobody knew where she was? Charlie was dead, and she was the only person in the world who knew the truth. Eadgyth would find the treasure and be away from the island before the monks had even set out, and then they would kill her to stop her talking! She was quite alone and there was no one to save her but herself.

Stretching her fingers, she pressed her bleeding wrists against the coarse rope that chafed her flesh. Her wrists and ankles had swollen as she'd struggled against the ropes. Out of the corner of her eye, Marian glimpsed a pile of razor shells, slim and straight and tantalizingly out of reach. Cautiously, she began to rock her way towards them, worming painfully across the stony cave floor.

Reaching the shells was just the beginning. Only the memory of the old man's skinny hands as he held the twisted knife to her throat kept her going, rubbing, rubbing against the sharp edge of the shell, until painfully slowly the fibres began to unravel. Hours passed before the frayed ends of the rope finally gave way, and Marian's inflamed wrists sprang apart. She wrenched off the filthy gag and wiped her gritty mouth with the back of a bloodstained hand. Then, turning to her ankles, she began to ease the tight knots with stiff, cold fingers.

Free at last, Marian stood up cautiously, scanning the gloomy cave for any sign of life, flexing her poor mangled feet. She could barely see as she hobbled around the dying fire, groping her way soundlessly around an outcrop of rock, only to discover that it led her deeper into the hermit's lair. She drew quickly back into the shadows in alarm. A smaller cave had opened out in front of her. Black candles guttered in the stale air.

As she turned to retrace her steps she heard a sudden noise behind her. Her own wild scream rang in her ears as she fled in panic, sensing the hermit close behind. She could hear his ragged breath rattling in his throat, crabs'-claw feet scrabbling over the gritty floor.

In the half-light before dawn, thin fingers of light were feeling their way down into the cave. Just as she turned to begin the climb, she felt a scabby hand close around her ankle. Her feet skidded on the slippery stone and she was down, fighting for her life on the rocky ledge, the hermit astride her back. She could feel his bony knees digging into her spine; surely he weighed no more than a sparrow and yet he had the strength of an ox. Her head dangled over the ledge's rim and she closed her eyes against the dizzying drop to the cruel rocks below. Summoning all her strength she flung herself furiously upwards, banging the back of her head against his face. The hermit shrieked in pain as he bit his tongue, leaping backwards, giving Marian the chance to scramble away from the edge of the precipice. She spun round giddily, trying to stand, but her enemy was behind her. Roaring in triumph he aimed his final kick. Instinctively she flung herself to one side and covered her face with her hands. The hermit's foot met only empty space, and the force of his lunge propelled him over the edge. His screams were truly terrible; cries of rage and fear as he fell like a broken doll, down, down on to the jagged rocks.

In the misty dawn light, Brother Dominic was sure that he could see a figure on the cliff top. The monks' sturdy craft was nearing the beach as he paused in his rowing and peered towards the shore.

'Do you see that, Father Simeon?' he asked. 'Someone is waving frantically from the cliffs!'

Father Simeon narrowed his eyes. 'My sight is not what it once was, Brother Dominic, but I do believe it is Lady Marian. What in heaven's name is the matter with her? Lady Marian,' he cried, scrambling unsteadily to his feet, 'are you all right? Come down to the beach.' He beckoned, almost overbalancing in the boat. 'We have a surprise for you!'

'Simeon!' exclaimed Father Bernard crossly. 'Sit down,

please. You are behaving like a novice. Have a care or you will tip the surprise into the sea!'

'Father Bernard, Father Bernard, they've killed Charlie,' sobbed Marian, picking her way over the stones leading down to the beach, her matted hair hanging down like tangled seaweed around her bruised face. Her bare feet and hands were bleeding.

'Good God, my child, what has befallen you?' cried Father Bernard in alarm. 'Why is your face so lacerated? You look half crazed.'

Marian limped the last few yards and flung herself at Father Bernard, convulsed with sobs.

'I … I … don't know where they've taken his body, but Eadgyth hit him with a meat cleaver. They would have killed me too! They were planning to but –'

Marian let out a shriek of terror as she recognized Eadgyth and Brother Gilbert in the fishing boat.

'It's them! It's them, Father Bernard!' she screamed, clutching his cloak. 'They murdered Charlie!'

'Peace, Marian, calm yourself,' urged Father Bernard, staring at the distraught girl with a puzzled frown. 'Charlie's not dead. We have him here in the boat.'

'N … not dead?' she cried. She stared at Father Bernard in disbelief, and then at the unconscious form of Charlie, pale as death in the stern of the boat, with Balthazar tucked in beside him, almost invisible against Father Bernard's sombre travelling cloak.

'You are mistaken, my dear,' said Father Simeon, looking bewildered. 'We found Charlie on the island.'

'And look, Marian,' said Father Bernard. 'We've found the treasure too!'

Marian gazed at the mound of treasure in the bottom of the boat in stunned silence.

'Poor Charlie,' was all she said.

'What's that noise, Simeon?' asked Father Bernard, putting a comforting arm around Marian's shivering shoulders.

A distant thrumming could be heard, borne on the breeze from the castle courtyard where a crowd was gathering in the early morning light.

'It must be the drums, Bernard. The villain Sturgeon is due to be executed at sunrise. I don't know how all this fits together, but these scoundrels in the boat will have some questions to answer too, before the sun goes down.'

'Sturgeon!' gasped Marian, clapping her hand to her mouth. 'But of course – how could you possibly know?'

'Know what, my dear?' asked Father Simeon gently.

'Sturgeon is innocent!' cried Marian. 'He has nothing to do with the murder at all!' She looked around at the monks desperately. 'Somebody's got to stop them! Did you say sunrise?' she moaned, squinting out to sea in panic. As they all turned to stare towards the horizon, the waves began to glimmer with the first weak rays of the rising sun.

38
Execution

The smell of fried pork wafted across to the dungeons from the castle kitchens. Sturgeon, deep in his underground cell, was sobbing. The bruises on his face were fading from livid purple to yellows and greens.

'That fried pork needs more seasoning,' he wailed. 'I can tell from the smell of it. Oh, what will poor Lady Goslar do without her Sturgeon?'

He heard the crunch of the gaoler's great iron key in the lock.

'Come on, you old rascal, let's get them leg irons off ya. Chop chop. Heh heh. D'ya get it? Hurry up. Chop chop? Oh, never mind! It's time to go.'

In the main castle courtyard the executioner was putting the finishing touches to the block. The drums began to beat, a dull rhythmic thudding in the misty dawn. Groups were gathering in the courtyard, bowmen and huntsmen, grooms and falconers, musicians and laundry maids. They had all risen early to watch Sturgeon go to the scaffold.

'I'm a hangman by profession you know,' the executioner chortled to one of the grooms as he sharpened his axe. 'Never done a beheading before! I've seen 'em done, but I've never actually performed one meself! Old Sturgeon's got a mighty thick neck. I'm gonna need a right hefty swipe to get it all off in one go,' he muttered, testing the blade of the axe with a horny thumb.

'So sorry to be late, everyone,' puffed Lord Goslar, waddling up the rickety steps to the temporary platform. 'Lady Goslar had hidden my ceremonial robes in the hopes of stopping the execution. She is distraught, poor love – beside herself with grief.'

He glanced anxiously towards Lady Goslar's empty window.

'I told my little pudding not to watch,' he said bitterly. 'It will quite spoil her appetite!'

The drums rolled to a crescendo before stopping abruptly. The sound of clanking chains could be heard getting steadily nearer. Supported by the gaoler, Sturgeon stumbled pathetically into the courtyard, dragging one bloody foot behind him. Passing by the raised platform, he lifted his great head and fixed Lord Goslar with a grim stare. Lord Goslar glowered back reproachfully before turning his back on the humbled master chef.

'I don't know what he's looking so glum about,' grumbled Lord Goslar. 'It should have been a hanging, only Lady Goslar wouldn't hear of it. He's getting a proper nobleman's death!'

'Here at last, eh?' chuckled the headsman. He gave Sturgeon a friendly shove. Sturgeon's body quivered, but he made no reply.

'Oh, well, don't cost yer nothin' to be polite, I always say.'

The drums began to beat again as Lord Goslar rose to his feet. Perspiration was dripping from his brow, though the morning air was icy cold.

'If ya wouldn't mind just putting yer head on this 'ere block, mister. Now, I'd better tell ya – I've not exactly done this before, but I have had a little practice on some of me mum's chickens!'

The drums were beating more slowly now and the crowd had fallen silent. Lord Goslar raised his hand.

'It gives me no pleasure,' he shouted across the heads of the eager crowd, 'to order the execution this morning of our master chef, Theophilus Sturgeon.' Rich smells of gravy and freshly baked bread filled the courtyard. 'Sturgeon was a cook of the highest calibre, an original and creative genius.'

A mixture of cheers and boos rose up from the crowd.

'But my duty is plain. Good citizens of Goslar Castle – the condemned man has been fairly tried by ordeal and found guilty of the most monstrous crimes – poisoning and murder! He has proved unworthy of our most sacred trust. It is nevertheless …' he glanced nervously up at his wife's chamber window, 'with the greatest regret and sense of profound betrayal that I order that his head and body be severed one from the other!'

The crowd yelled its approval as hats were flung in the air. The headsman heaved the blade back behind his shoulder. The crowd held its breath. A raven cawed in the still, frosty air. The monastery bell began to toll mournfully.

'Stop! Stop! Lord Goslar, I beseech you!'

Father Bernard came skidding into the courtyard clutching his chest with the effort of running, pressing at a stabbing pain that ripped through his side. 'There's been a terrible mistake! You've got the wrong man. Lord Goslar, you must stop this execution immediately! Sturgeon is innocent!'

The crowd erupted in indignation as Lady Goslar flew into the courtyard behind Father Bernard in a riot of yellow petticoats.

'Godfrey, oh, Godfrey. Stop! I saw Father Bernard running towards the castle from the gallery window. He told me to rush down here and stop you. Oh, Father, there you are! You beat me to it. Thank God! Heaven be praised. Has Father Bernard told you the wonderful news? Sturgeon is innocent!'

Sturgeon had not moved; his head remained on the executioner's block, still awaiting the expected blow. Lady Goslar waddled over to him, flinging herself down on the ground beside her chief cook.

'Sturgeon, oh, you poor man, can you hear me? What have the brutes done to you? It's going to be all right now. We know you are innocent!'

'But they've left out the parsley,' he whimpered. 'I can smell it from here. They've left out the parsley!'

'Guards! Take the condemned man back to the cells until I decide what to do with him,' barked Lord Goslar in confusion.

'Not back to the cells,' wailed Lady Goslar. 'Didn't you hear what Father Bernard said? He's innocent, the poor man! Just look at the state he's in. Guards, fetch a stretcher and take this poor innocent to the infirmary. Father Bernard! Is that old goat still alive, you know, the one that knows all about herbs and such? You know, that monk that's nearly a hundred.'

'Er, Lord Goslar, if I might interrupt for just a moment,' began Father Bernard. 'You will be relieved to know that Lady Marian is safe. She has had a terrifying ordeal.'

'Lady Marian?' said Lord Goslar, looking more bewildered than ever. 'What has Lady Marian got to do with anything? What do you mean, she's safe? Where has she been? Nobody knew she was missing!'

Charlie's eyes glittered feverishly in the dark-yellow candle flame. He moaned feebly, kicking off his blankets. Balthazar sprang from the window sill and leapt lightly on to the bed, his usually sleek fur bedraggled and unkempt. He was carrying something delicately in his mouth. He dropped it gently on to the pillow next to Charlie's matted blond hair. Retracting his claws, he passed a velvet paw over the boy's sleeping face.

'Wake up,' he whispered, bringing his mouth close to Charlie's. 'I've found some prunella – the carpenter's herb. Charlie! Wake up!'

'Balthazar,' he groaned, stretching out a feeble hand to touch the cat's damp fur. 'Where am I? I feel so ill.' He started up, staring wildly around him, clutching his head as a burning pain shot behind his eyes.

'Listen, Charlie. The monks can't help you here. Father Simeon means well but his ideas are so primitive and your wound smells revolting! Look, I've found some of the self-heal plant your mother used to use, the carpenter's herb. If that wound's not treated properly soon you … you could die! It's going bad.'

'I've never felt so sick in all my life, Balthazar,' groaned Charlie, a tear forming in the corner of his eye. 'I'm so afraid of dying … away from home –'

'You're not going to die, Charlie!' said Balthazar fiercely, his emerald eyes glittering with a cold fire. 'I promised your mother I'd look after you and I never break my word.'

He nudged the small green plant with his paw, releasing a pungent smell from its dark pointed leaves. The door opened suddenly. Balthazar darted under the bed.

'Oh, good,' said Father Simeon encouragingly. 'You're awake. I've prepared a syrup of … oh, what's this?' he said, picking up the herb from Charlie's bolster. 'Mmmm,' he grunted approvingly, his nostrils flaring. 'What a delicious odour. I wonder where this came from.'

39
Sailing West

'The Carpenter's Herb,' mumbled Father Simeon happily, scratching away at the parchment with his quill pen. He blew on the ink before tying the newly inscribed label around the rim of an earthenware jar. 'A miraculous plant – quite spectacular!'

Father Bernard popped his head around the door of the pharmacy.

'Are you talking to yourself in there, Simeon?'

'Come along in, Bernard,' he said, smiling brightly. 'I have just finished potting up the last batch of the paste that was so efficacious in healing Charlie's wounds. A most exciting new cure and one that I will find very useful.'

'Indeed. The boy has made a wonderful recovery. It is hard to believe that he was so ill just two weeks ago. But what do you make of him, Simeon? Has he told you any of his strange stories? Do you believe that he is a wanderer in time or does he just have a vivid imagination?'

Father Simeon trotted over to a wide shelf and placed the

freshly labelled jar next to a row of identical ones.

'He is a remarkably intelligent boy,' he replied, smiling. 'I am delighted that we were able to remove him from the kitchens and give him a home here in the monastery.'

'Oh, I know he is intelligent, Simeon. His Latin translations are excellent and he is making sound progress with Greek too, but I am nonetheless greatly troubled about him. Although his tales are fascinating to say the least, I do not want to encourage him to live in a fantasy world.'

'I do not believe that he does, Bernard. It is you, I am afraid, my friend, who has too little imagination. The world is full of wonders. I am inclined to believe every word he says, remarkable though it may seem. The boy is a marvel, a treasure trove of fascinating and advanced new medical ideas.'

'And not just medical ideas, Simeon. You won't believe what he told me the other day. He said that people in his time truly believe that the earth is round! He actually told me that some explorers had sailed west to try to get to the east!'

Father Simeon looked aghast.

'I know what you mean, Bernard. Some of his tales are a bit far-fetched and, I might add, positively dangerous.' Father Simeon leaned towards Father Bernard and whispered in his ear. 'He was telling me the other day that some people where he comes from believe that the earth is not the centre of the universe!'

Father Bernard gasped in disbelief, paling visibly.

'I know Bernard – shocking isn't it? But he is only young after all. I told him that he must put silly notions like that right out of his head or he could get into serious trouble.'

'Has he spoken to you of his home?' asked Father Bernard uneasily.

'Oh, yes indeed, Bernard. I have heard all about his mother and her miraculous healing powers. I have filled pages of parchment with details of cures that Charlie has explained to me. I thought at first that she must be an eminent doctor in his time, but it seems she is only some kind of village wise woman! I find that very hard to believe.'

'But his tales are so outlandish. How can you be convinced they are true?'

'He could never have made it all up, you know,' said Father Simeon, 'about that king with the six wives who kept chopping their heads off and the weapons that spit fire and metal and kill the enemy at great distances.'

Father Bernard nodded, scratching his tonsure. 'In any event I am worried about him. He is certainly well and strong again in body, and yet he seems unsettled and troubled in his mind. Over the last few days he has seemed less and less able to concentrate on his studies, easily distracted and moody.'

'Perhaps he is simply homesick, Bernard. As I told you, I truly believe he is a wandering spirit, lost and far from his family.'

Charlie sat dreamily at the library window looking out over the calm sea far below. It was a perfect day. A tiny figure in a peacock-blue gown was sauntering along the beach, a rangy grey deerhound running along in front of her, splashing in the shallows.

'Marian!' shouted Charlie out of the window.

'Sshh!' exclaimed a monk crossly, staring at a blob of

unwanted scarlet paint on the manuscript he was decorating.
'You startled me.'

'Sorry. I didn't mean to make you jump.'

'You'd better warn me next time you're going to bellow like that,' he complained grumpily, blotting at the stain with a piece of linen.

Charlie turned back to the window. 'Marian!' he called, only slightly more quietly.

She looked up, shading her eyes with her hand, scanning the arched openings. She began to wave madly, shouting something he couldn't make out. Otto started up a wild barking, chasing his tail round and round in excitement.

'Stay where you are,' called Charlie. 'I'm coming down.'

He jumped up from his desk, carefully placing a marker in the medical book that he had been reading, and tiptoed noisily out of the library to a chorus of shushing. Nearing the door, he broke into a run, sweeping up his cloak from the row of hooks as he sped past and down the wide stone steps.

As he drew level with Marian on the beach, Otto leapt up at him, trying to wash Charlie's face with his huge pink tongue.

'There's no one he likes as much as you, Charlie,' laughed Marian, tossing a piece of driftwood out into the waves for Otto to fetch. 'Ever since you saved him from that ghastly mandrake root!'

Charlie shivered. 'Thank goodness we've seen the last of that evil old hermit. Heaven knows what they were planning to do with the mandrake!'

Marian shuddered. 'I know – all those roots hanging up to dry like little old men. Ugh, I'll never forget that ghastly cave as long as I live.'

'What are you doing out here on the beach?' asked Charlie, hastily changing the subject. He hugged his cloak around him. 'The sea looks tempting from a distance, but it's freezing.'

'I had to get out. You'd never believe the commotion in the castle, and it's entirely your fault! It's all right for you – you can escape to the monastery.'

'What do you mean, my fault? What have I done?'

'The feast, you fathead. It's all in your honour – well, yours and Sturgeon's.'

Charlie groaned. 'I feel such a fool, you know – having a feast held in my honour!' He sighed, skimming a flat pebble skilfully over the frothy waves.

'Will you teach me to do that?' asked Marian, impressed. 'Perhaps in the summer when the weather turns warmer?'

Charlie looked at her sadly. He hadn't dared to broach the subject with Marian, but he had a distinct feeling his time with her was running out. He was happy with the monks, but he knew he couldn't stay on here for ever. He was restless. How did Balthazar describe the feeling? Fidgety and off his food – that was it. And he needed to know what had happened to his mother, even if it was bad news.

'I don't think you've been listening to a word I've just said,' complained Marian crossly.

'Oh, sorry, Marian. I was, er … just thinking about my Latin translation for Father Bernard,' he gabbled hurriedly. 'I can't seem to concentrate on my studies these days.'

'Nor can I,' agreed Marian, 'but then of course I never could!'

40
Songbird Pie

The pastry cooks were in despair. Yet another failure! The piecrust looked just right, but when they cut it open, only one poor bedraggled blackbird staggered out, his companions limp and suffocated under the broken crust.

'What!' roared Sturgeon, now fully recovered from his brief spell in the castle dungeons. 'Don't say they're dead again, you idiots! I told you – it couldn't be simpler. The pie needs to be cooked slowly, but not too slowly or the birds will get drowsy and won't fly out when the pie's cut. It needs to be cooked quickly, but not too quickly or the pastry will burn and the birds will be charred to cinders. The crust should be crisp, but not too crisp or they won't be able to burst their way through. Listen to me, you nincompoops! Lady Goslar has ordered a live-songbird pie for the feast and a live-songbird pie she's gonna have!'

Charlie couldn't decide what to wear for the banquet. Lord

Goslar had sent him a selection of brightly coloured robes to choose from and he'd reluctantly selected the emerald-green velvet slashed with crimson silk. He looked like a jester!

There was a knock at the door, and a novice in a plain grey habit poked his head around the frame. 'Er, sorry to interrupt,' he said, suppressing a smirk, 'but Father Bernard wants to see you in his study before the feast – as soon as you're ready.'

Charlie grimaced. He still hadn't finished that Latin translation. He rushed to gather up the scattered pieces of parchment, tripping over the hem of his robe in his hurry. He followed the novice down the stone steps, feeling like a gaudy bird chasing a grey moth.

He had expected to find Father Bernard alone. Abbot Gregory smiled kindly at him from under his shaggy black brows as Father Bernard strode forward to greet him.

'Come in, Charlie. My word! Don't you look grand?'

He held Charlie at arm's length to get a better look. Charlie was blushing furiously.

'Sit down, my child,' said Father Bernard. 'Thank you for coming so promptly on your special evening. Abbot Gregory and I wanted to have a little chat with you before the Feast of the Treasure.'

'If it's about the Latin translation, Father –'

Father Bernard waved his hand dismissively. 'Put the parchment down, Charlie. It's nothing to do with Latin.'

'Father Bernard has been singing your praises to me,' complimented the abbot. 'He tells me you are a gifted Latin scholar and not at all bad at Greek either. Now, Father Bernard and all the monks are most grateful to you for helping us to uncover the odious poisoner and to restore the priceless treasure to the abbey.'

'Oh, that was nothing, Father,' he grinned, pleased to be praised by the abbot.

'Nothing, my child? You led us to the ring,' said Abbot Gregory. 'You solved the riddle and exposed the murderer! We would never have found the treasure without you. You are too modest, but then modesty is a great gift. You are blessed with many talents, Charlie, which brings me to the reason for this meeting.'

'Now, Charlie,' continued Father Bernard at a nod from the abbot, 'we know only a little of your past, about your previous life in another place, and, er … maybe even in another time. We don't pretend to understand it at all, but we do feel that you are a talented boy with certain, how shall I put it – special powers. Abbot Gregory and I have discussed your position at length. It is rather irregular having you living with us in the monastery and yet not quite belonging to our brotherhood.'

'The fact is, Charlie,' interrupted the abbot, 'that we would like to offer you a permanent home here with us in the monastery. We are inviting you to become a novice, to exchange …' he looked at Charlie's vibrant green robe with a twinkle in his eye, 'the green for the grey!'

Charlie gazed down at his crimson slippers. There was a lump in his throat.

'We think you would make a fine monk of the scholarly type; perhaps even become a doctor. Father Simeon is most impressed with your superior knowledge of medicine and herbs.'

There was a silence, broken only by the shifting of brushwood on the fire. Charlie was touched. He'd been contented with the monks – eccentric and kindly Father Simeon, and Father Bernard who was quite as good a tutor as Father Hubert. Yes, it could be a good life, a safe and scholarly one. But it was not his life; he didn't belong here. He had to find out what had happened to his mother. For all he knew she might already be dead, killed by the mob as a witch, but then again, maybe not. How could he reply to the abbot's kind offer?

'We understand that it cannot be an easy decision for you,' said Father Bernard, sensing his unease. 'Think it over. The feast will be starting soon, and it is held in your honour don't forget. But before you go off to the revels, the abbot has something for you – a little gift.'

Abbot Gregory picked up a package from the table next to him. He turned it over in his hands hesitantly before passing it to Charlie.

'Open it, Charlie,' said Father Bernard softly.

Charlie's fingers fumbled with a silken cord tied around a small bulky object wrapped in violet silk. There in the folds lay the cross of Saint Oswald, the one that had saved his life but … this one was perfect! Charlie was dumbstruck. He had the other one, broken and smashed in two by Eadgyth's meat cleaver, safe in his room.

'Surprised?' smiled Father Bernard.

'But how … how has it been mended? No, it can't have been repaired – it's safe in my –'

'No, Charlie, it has not been mended. It would take a goldsmith of great skill to repair that mangled object. No, this is another one that Abbot Gregory and I found among the chalices and golden plate that was discovered on the island. However, we are sure that it is identical to the one that saved your life. And look – it has some lettering on the reverse side.'

Charlie felt light-headed. The candlelight gleamed on the cross, illuminating the initials of his name – C.F. 'But …?'

'Strange, is it not, Charlie? Your own initials inscribed on the Saxon cross found in the hoard of treasure, and the cross identical in every respect to the one that saved your life.'

Charlie gazed incredulously at the abbot. 'Take it – it is yours,' he said. 'Wear it with pride.'

'But I can't keep it,' gasped Charlie. 'It's much too precious.'

'Take it, my child,' urged the abbot. 'It was meant for you – of that I am sure.' He stood up, smiling. 'Now, run along or you'll be late for the banquet. But don't forget our offer, Charlie. We believe you would make a very fine novice, but the choice is yours.'

41
Novice or Squire?

The feast was in full swing. Charlie sat in the seat of honour next to Lord Goslar. Marian, almost pretty in her saffron gown, was enjoying herself more than she had expected.

'Now, Charlie, my lad,' said Lord Goslar, wiping gravy from his beard with his sleeve. 'I've been thinking. You're a sturdy boy. I don't have a son of my own, you know, a boy who I could train up as a squire. So perhaps I could train you up … you know … teach you to hunt, instruct you in the arts of war … hawking, jousting, archery. You could even train your own kestrel. What do you say?'

'Erm, well … that's very thoughtful of you, sir, but I –'

'Oh, don't thank me, Charlie! It is the very least that I can offer you – after all you have done for us!'

Charlie bit his lip. What an evening! First an invitation to become a novice, and now a squire! He had the new cross of Saint Oswald, the perfect one bearing the initials C.F., safe around his neck under his robe. It filled him with a warm glow. A fanfare of trumpets sounded.

'The songbird pie!' squealed Lady Goslar. 'I do hope Sturgeon has managed to get it right.'

Charlie had had enough revelry for one evening. He felt detached, as if watching the merriment from a distance – through the wrong end of a spyglass. He was not looking forward to the next part of the celebrations – the speeches about him from Lord Goslar, the adulation. He felt tired of it all and strangely lonely.

The songbird pie was presented to Lord Goslar, its golden crust glowing in the candlelight. It was hard to hear much amid the gasps from the expectant guests, but Charlie was sure he could just detect a faint twittering sound. Lord Goslar rose to his feet brandishing a silver knife.

'Oh, do get on with it, Godfrey,' squealed Lady Goslar. 'I can hear the birds a-squeaking inside!' She lunged for the knife and plunged it deep into the yellow crust. All at once there came a twittering and a squawking, as in a rush of wings and feathers the live birds burst through the piecrust, sending chunks of pastry and feathers flying in all directions. Everyone ducked as the terrified birds swooped in panic, knocking over tankards and snuffing out candles. The hall was plunged into sudden darkness.

'It's worked, it's worked!' screamed Lady Goslar. She was on her feet clapping her hands in delight. 'It's a triumph!'

'Oh, the poor things,' wailed Marian. 'They're scared witless.'

One by one the candles were rekindled in their iron stands. The songbirds were perched along the rafters, some with singed wings but most none the worse for their ordeal.

Marian, who had covered her eyes in disgust, peered round at Charlie. 'Ugh, wasn't that revolting?'

But Charlie's seat was empty. Her friend had gone.

Charlie's fuddled head cleared quickly. It was bitterly cold outside after the warmth of sweaty bodies and roaring fires. He could still hear raucous laughter spilling from the Great Hall as he crossed the barren scrubby ground towards the monastery. He felt a familiar pressure on his leg.

'Hello, Balthazar. What are you up to?'

'Same as you, I should say – wondering what I'm going to do next. Time to go home, I think. I can feel it in my whiskers. I've had the sensation for a day or two now. I'm not my usual self – you know the kind of thing – off my food, bilious, unsettled.'

'But we can't just choose to go home when we like. You told me that yourself,' said Charlie with a worried frown.

'Oh, yes – that's true enough. The time chooses us, not we the time,' said Balthazar mysteriously.

'But how can we be sure we'll get home, anyway? We could end up somewhere worse. I'm not unhappy here. If I can't be at home, there isn't anywhere else I'd rather be. Look, Balthazar, I'm just calling in on Father Simeon. You'd better make yourself scarce for a bit. You know he doesn't like animals in the infirmary.'

Charlie could see a light in the pharmacy. Father Simeon

must still be up. The oak door was closed and Charlie knocked softly.

'Father Simeon – it's me – Charlie.'

He heard the iron bolt slide back. A slice of light expanded on the path.

'Come in, come in, my boy! Shouldn't you be at the feast?'

The room was warm and smoky, smelling strongly of herbs. Father Simeon had a good fire burning in the hearth, his cauldron simmering over it as usual.

'Oh, I just slipped out for a breath of fresh air – to have a bit of a think. What are you doing, Father?'

'Just pottering about, my dear, making up lists for the spring. It has been a long cold winter and I have used up a lot of vital ingredients.'

Charlie looked at Father Simeon's spidery brown writing in the guttering candlelight. 'Boar's urine? How on earth do you manage to get that?'

'With great difficulty, Charlie, but it is most efficacious when you can get it. When mixed with hog's grease it is marvellous against the rotting of the gums, and when taken inwardly, it is a powerful cure for constipation!'

'And what's in the cauldron?'

'Ah, now this is interesting.' Father Simeon trotted over to the pot and gave it a stir. 'Monks' rhubarb. It's a new remedy I'm trying out for worms. I've used the juice before, which mixed with vinegar is a wonderful cure for indigestion, and, er, flatulence.'

'Flatulence?' Charlie's mind was full of home and Father Hubert. He smiled to himself. 'Do you have any of that to spare, Father?'

'Oh, to be sure. I've jars of the stuff. Here – take some. Now, sit down, my boy. You look uncomfortable shuffling about there. Is something wrong?'

'Abbot Gregory wants me to become a novice,' he blurted out, 'and … and Lord Goslar wants me to train as a squire and –'

'And you want to go home. I know, Charlie. I've sensed it for days now.'

'I feel confused, Father. Everybody's been so kind to me. Father Bernard is the best Latin teacher I've ever had, and I love discussing medicine here with you, and then there's Marian …' he trailed off. 'That's the worst of it. What can I say to Marian?'

'Charlie.' Father Simeon grasped his arm firmly. 'You are a sensitive boy with a warm kind spirit, but you can't please everybody, you know. You might try to, but you will never succeed. You must have courage, Charlie, and follow your heart in all things – and your heart, I believe, lies at home.'

Charlie sighed. He pulled out some pieces of parchment from his pocket, labelled in his none too tidy handwriting: Abbot Gregory, Father Bernard, Marian, Barnacle. He held them out to Father Simeon. He couldn't speak, his eyes were blurred with tears and his throat ached.

Father Simeon took them in his frail old hand. 'I'll deliver them to your friends, my child,' he said gently. 'Don't you worry. Everyone will understand in time, even Marian.'

'Oh, and this is for Marian too,' said Charlie shakily. He fumbled in his pocket again and drew out a little bag smelling of cloves. 'It's a charm bag – for lasting friendship. Tell her ... tell her there's one for her and one for me. I'll always carry mine.'

Father Simeon nodded, taking the package.

'I've ... I've nothing for you, Father. I couldn't think of anything you needed.' He looked around the small pharmacy, its shelves piled high with jars and bottles. 'I don't want to be a novice and I don't want to be a squire. I want to be a doctor, just like you, Father Simeon. That's what I've decided. You're a wonderful healer. If I live to be ninety, maybe I'll end up as good as you.'

Father Simeon squeezed his hand. 'I pray you will have a long and useful life, my child. But don't forget what I've often told you – you will live longer on the right diet. I don't know why people are dying so young these days! After all, Adam lived to be nine hundred and thirty years old. Now, run along, Charlie, and remember – always follow your heart.'

The door closed. Father Simeon sighed deeply and wiped a tear away with the back of his hand. 'Goodbye, Charlie,' he said softly to the oaken door. He took a deep breath and closed his eyes. 'Don't be such a sentimental old fool, Simeon. You've only got a few days left to live yourself! Now, what's that young rascal been up to this time?'

He turned over the piece of parchment addressed to Barnacle and began to read. 'Well of all the ...' he spluttered. 'The young scamp ...' He began to laugh. 'A love bath for Barnacle!' he read aloud. 'To make a person irresistible – mix rosemary and thyme in an earthenware jug with powdered roots of orris and lovage. Pour all over the body.' He opened Marian's note. 'A cure for nail biting! I think I'd better not look at Abbot Gregory's message,' he chuckled. 'I might discover something he'd prefer me not to know!'

42
Monks' Rhubarb

The cold moonlight shone through the window above Saint Oswald's tomb. Father Simeon's words echoed in Charlie's ears. *Have courage. Follow your heart.* He closed his eyes and took a deep breath. His hand closed around the golden cross beneath his emerald robe. Balthazar was on his shoulder, breathing rhythmically, trembling with suppressed tension. Charlie sank his fingers into Balthazar's warm fur. He could feel the now familiar tremor of sparks begin to shiver down his back. And suddenly they were falling – spiralling downwards, gathering speed, plummeting into the heart of a whirlwind. There was a rush of air in his ears, the babble of voices; dark and light, heat and cold. Down, down they fell through the ages, slipping in and out of the cracks in time.

Father Hubert breathed in the heavy scent of incense and golden beeswax as he lumbered down the nave of the parish church. A hungry rumble escaped from his stomach. There was just time for some cheese and ale before starting his daily visits to the sick. He frowned. Eating in the vestry always reminded him of young Charlie Ferret. They had shared bread and cheese together that last evening in October, the night before the boy had disappeared.

He was lowering himself down on to the little vestry stool when he heard a crash, followed by a cry and the mewling of a cat. He sprang clumsily to his feet, dropping his platter. The noise had come from the church.

Charlie fingered his bruised temple gently. He'd hit it hard on the end of a pew as he'd landed. Balthazar lay sprawled on the floor next to him, his claws extended, fur on end.

'Where are we this time?' moaned Charlie.

'Where do you think we are, idiot? I'd know that fat bottom anywhere!'

Charlie gasped. 'Father Hubert!'

The plump priest spun round in amazement. 'Charlie Ferret! Where are you? I can hear your voice but I can't see you anywhere.'

'I'm down here.' Charlie scrambled to his feet, tripping over his emerald robe. He emerged from between the pews, looking pale and shaken.

'Where have you been, Charlie, and what in heaven's name are you wearing? Travelling with a troop of actors or something? I heard a noise and I … Charlie? Are you all right, you look white as a …! Oh, Lord, I think he's going to faint – better get the boy some ale.'

'Now, I'm sure you can manage a morsel of cheese, Charlie,' urged Father Hubert with his mouth full. 'It's your favourite.'

'No, Father, honestly. I've just eaten – a banquet actually, held in my honour! It's a long story – I don't know where to begin ...' he stammered. All he really wanted was some news of his mother. He took a deep breath.

'Er, Father Hubert ...'

'I've never been more pleased to see anyone in my whole life.' The parish priest munched happily. 'I can't imagine where you've been, but explanations can wait until later. Right now, I think you should go and see your mother. She's been worried sick – quite given up hope. Nobody could blame you for going off that day, Charlie, but –'

'Mother!' Relief flooded in like a draught of sweet wine. 'She escaped the witch-finder after all? But how?'

'Oh, she didn't escape,' said Father Hubert, puffing out his cheeks. 'He got her, all right. It was a mighty close shave. She was captured on the day of the Feast Day Fair, the day you, er ... er ... disappeared.'

'So how come she's still alive? Is she all right? What did they do to her? She is all right, isn't she?'

'Don't look so worried, Charlie. She's alive and well, believe me – never been better, not since your father died, anyway. She's quite famous in these parts again; everyone's flocking to her since the trial – can't get enough of her cures. But she's out of her mind with worry about you.'

'So how –'

'It happened like this,' said Father Hubert with a twinkle in his eye. 'We had a stroke of good fortune. They've devised a new way of trying witches – none of those ducking stools any more. This new method involves two chairs – like a pair of scales. Two huge old family Bibles are placed on one chair and the unfortunate accused sits on the other.'

'I can't bear to think about it,' he said uneasily. 'What did they do to her? What happened?'

'Well, if the accused weighs less than the two great Bibles put together, they say it points to guilt. Since most of the so-called witches are poor wizened old women, they scarcely weigh more than a sparrow. That way they're all found guilty.'

'But Mother – she'd grown so thin and frail …'

'Thin and frail maybe, Charlie, but not stupid. Nobody could ever accuse Agnes Ferret of that, and I'm not so dim either. By good fortune, I was given the job of providing the Bibles for the trial.'

He heaved himself up from the stool, and unlocked a small trunk.

'Have a peep at this – but not a word to a soul, mind,' he muttered, handing Charlie a huge Bible, bound in black leather and fastened with a gilded clasp. He selected another key.

Charlie opened the book cautiously, as if it might bite him. 'But it's –'

'Empty!' Father Hubert beamed proudly. 'That's just it – weighs a lot less without its pages!'

Charlie laughed. 'But you've done it so neatly, just cut out a chunk from the centre and left a margin all around the edge. Nobody would ever know unless they –'

'Not unless they looked, Charlie,' grinned Father Hubert, 'and they can't do that without the key!' He replaced the key deep within the pocket of his robes. 'I can tell you, my heart was in my mouth at the trial. It was I who placed the books on the scales. I made a great show of staggering under their weight. You didn't know I was an actor, did you?'

'You're amazing, Father. You were risking your own life too.'

Father Hubert flushed with pleasure.

'Oh, it was nothing really. You know how I disapprove of this craze for finding sorcery in anyone slightly out of the ordinary. Anyway, it wasn't just the Bibles that saved her. She'd sewn stones into the lining of her cloak. As I said, your mother's nobody's fool! It was a heart-stopping moment, I can tell you, Charlie, but remember this: have the courage to do what is right and fear no man.'

'What did you say, Father Hubert?' said Charlie, startled.

'Oh, just a saying of my favourite saint – Saint Oswald of Northumbria – the owner of the holy hand, you know.'

Charlie fingered the golden cross on his chest thoughtfully. He beamed at the young priest. 'Well, I think you're one of the bravest people I know, Father. How can I ever thank you for saving Mother's life? It's wonderful to see you. I've got so much to tell you – things you won't believe.'

'And I can't wait to hear them, Charlie. Something tells me you've been at more than a fancy-dress party!'

Charlie looked down at his bright-green robe. 'Oh, I almost forgot. I've brought a present for you.'

He delved into his pocket, fumbling for the yellow jar. He held it out to Father Hubert, flushing slightly.

The priest twisted the pot between his fingers. 'Monks'-rhubarb-and-vinegar syrup – a cure for wind! Where in the world did you find this?'

'Oh, just a little potion I picked up on my travels. You never know – it might just do the trick.' He jumped up and glanced around for Balthazar. The cat was standing by the open church door, his tail twitching impatiently. 'Thanks for the ale, Father. I'll be over to see you later, but right now, I think my mother's in for a big surprise!'